Grant Grade School

District No. 33

979

Famous
Fairy Tales

Famous Fairy Tales

by Charles Perrault

pictures by Charles Mozley

TRANSLATED BY SARAH CHOKLA GROSS

A KEITH JENNISON BOOK
Franklin Watts, Inc., Publishers
A Division of Grolier Incorporated
575 Lexington Avenue, New York, N.Y. 10022

CONTENTS

About this Book

THINK of it, until the appearance of Perrault's *Contes*, nobody had ever read a fairy story! Plenty of people had *heard* fairy stories, for they were always told by one generation to the next. But it was not until Perrault wrote these stories down that they could read and enjoy them as we do today.

Charles Perrault was born in Paris on the 12th of January in the year 1628. He was one of four brothers, and his home was a comfortable one, for his father was a successful lawyer. Charles was sent to be educated at Beauvais, but did not get on well there, so he went to other schools, finally graduating in law at Orleans.

When Charles Perrault was twenty-three he became a lawyer in Paris, but he did not practise there long, for three years later he became clerk to his brother, who was head of the internal department for Paris. Ten years later he gave up this position and went to work for Jean Baptiste Colbert, the great French statesman. Charles Perrault's first job was to supervise the building of the French Observatory, then to be controller of royal buildings and to help found an academy of honors and medals. For this and other good work he was made a member of the French Academy. Then in 1683 Colbert died, and that was the end of Perrault's political career.

The years Perrault spent on his political career were important and exciting ones in France. The King was Louis the Fourteenth – a man whose wealth, power, military victories and dazzling Court caused Europe to nickname him "the Grand Monarch", or "the Sun King". He was a lover of elegance, splash, and luxury.

Louis had many fine homes but he wanted a personal palace in which to entertain his gay friends, so he built one outside Paris, at Versailles, with lovely avenues of trees leading to it, elaborate gardens with many formal flower beds and the prettiest fountains imaginable – to this day one of the world's most beautiful sights.

Louis the Fourteenth gathered round him the best playwrights of France – Corneille, Racine and Molière, and the poet La Fontaine. To amuse the Court, La Fontaine put into delightful verse his still-popular Aesop's Fables. Everyone laughed, and enjoyed the way these moral tales poked fun at Court life and situations.

Charles Perrault had always taken an interest in literature and was of course stimulated by the gay life around him. So when at the age of fifty-five he had nothing to do, he did exactly what many men retiring after distinguished careers do to-day: he became a writer. But he did not write his memoirs, as to-day's retired gentlemen usually do. Instead, he wrote fairy stories – three of them, in not very good verse. Fairy stories in bad verse were not considered worthy of a French Academician, so the critics wrote scornful reviews of them, which is perhaps one reason why, as you will read later, he did not want to put his name on another book.

Of the three stories in not-too-good verse, one – *The Three Wasted Wishes* – appears, in prose, in this book.

In 1697 the *Histoires ou Contes du temps passé* – stories or tales of long ago – which was subtitled *Mother Goose Tales (Contes de Ma Mère l'Oie)* – were first published. These were the eight stories that we have come to know so well: *Cinderella*, the *Sleeping Beauty*, *Hop o'my Thumb*, *Diamonds and Toads*, *Blue Beard*, *Puss-in-Boots*, *Little Red Riding Hood*, and *Ricky with a Tuft*.

Nobody knows who wrote these famous stories, for the editions published in Charles Perrault's lifetime are signed by the name of his young son, Pierre. It is more likely Charles wrote them, for Pierre never published anything else, and even though Charles was unwilling to use his own name, it seems to me probable that it was he who wrote these stories. If, however, you like to believe that Pierre, the son, wrote them, you can read the whole fascinating detective story in Percy Muir's *English Children's Books* (Praeger, 1953).

It is possible that Charles Perrault first heard these stories when they were told to his children by their nurse. This is suggested by the woodcut in the earliest editions, which shows an elderly woman with three children. This would account too for the shortness of the stories, as probably the old nurse trusted to the tones of her voice to bring the characters to life so she wasted no time on long telling. But the *Contes*, though written with a charming simplicity, are many of them sadly short, and leave the reader longing to know more. Perhaps that is why many other writers, especially Andrew Lang, have re-told these stories.

This Treasure Edition now in your hand has the true Perrault stories, but the translator has treated them like jewels whose beauty may be improved by resetting. As, for instance, in the story of Sleeping Beauty – which probably has its roots in mythology – Perrault wrote that the parents left the palace before sleep fell on their daughter and her household. Long ago children refused to accept so cruel a story, and have insisted on the King and Queen also sleeping for a hundred years, so in this book the King and Queen are there to greet their daughter when she wakes up. There are other touches which bring new brilliance to the old jewels. You will have fun discovering them. You will have fun too if you keep one eye on life in the reign of Louis the Fourteenth, for remember it was in that reign that these elegant stories were written.

The Sleeping Beauty

The Sleeping Beauty

ONCE upon a time there was a King and Queen who had almost every reason to be happy. The King was a young man, as kind and as wise as he was handsome. He had married the fairest of ladies for his Queen. They found great pleasure in one another, for they enjoyed the same music, savored the same dishes, and laughed at the same things.

But one sad lack marred their happiness: they had no child.

They so dearly wanted a child that they sought help from any source. They consulted oracles. They went

3

on pilgrimages. They said prayers and lit candles. They made vows. They tried everything, but their efforts seemed fruitless.

The day came, however, when to their great joy, the Queen gave birth to a daughter. Everyone felt happy. The King, from a balcony of the palace, smiled and bowed and waved to his cheering subjects. Small boys turned handsprings in the street. Parents hugged their own children. Far into the night, fireworks burst into showers of sparks against the sky. There was rejoicing in all parts of the kingdom.

The King and Queen decided to call their baby Princess after the earliest and loveliest part of the day – the dawn. So they named her *Aurora*, which means dawn. Then they set the time for a splendid christening.

The King rang for his Major-domo, and together they made two important lists. One list was of *Persons to be Invited*. The other was of *Things to Have Ready*. At the head of the list of persons to be invited were the seven beloved Fairies of the country – the only fairies known to be in the land. "And a very fortunate number it is, Sire," said the Major-domo. "Seven is considered lucky!" Each was to be a godmother to the baby Princess.

At the top of the list of things to have ready, coming before "Flags at windows", "Garlands to deck the halls", and "New red carpet for rolling out", the Major-domo wrote, "golden table-setting." For the King had ordered seven special plates and seven spoons, seven forks and seven knives to be made by the royal goldsmith just for the Fairy Godmothers. No one else had any like these – not even the King himself, nor his sweet Queen. The name of each Fairy was engraved on her plate.

It was understood that if the Fairy Godmothers each brought little Aurora a lifelong gift, as fairy godmothers always used to do for a godchild, she would then indeed be the best princess and the luckiest in the world.

On the day of the christening, after the baby Princess had been named, the Fairy guests and the court and ambassadors from neighboring kingdoms – and ordinary people too – everyone for miles around gathered with the King and Queen in the banquet room. At the very moment that the Fairies sat down at their places of honor set with the golden service, a bent figure in black suddenly appeared in the arched doorway.

It was the Oldest Fairy, scowling over her cane at

the suddenly quiet assemblage. She was so old that no one there had ever seen her, because for half a century she had lived high up in a tower, away from the world, forgotten.

The King and Queen had never even heard her name, so of course they had not been able to invite her, and of course they could not set before her an engraved plate of gold with a knife and fork and a jeweled spoon. Nonetheless, in perfect courtesy they bade her welcome to their table and seated her with the other Fairy Godmothers.

The Oldest Fairy sat down, but she looked scornfully at the china service at her place. She made it clear that she felt insulted because she had had no invitation to this high occasion, and because the other Fairies had special personally engraved plates with jeweled spoons. Under her breath – but loud enough for her anger to be known – she said ugly words.

One of the young Fairies, who sat nearest her, heard her mutterings and mumblings. She guessed that the old crone meant to punish the King and Queen for their accidental slight by making a wicked wish for the little Princess. Therefore, when the moment came for the Fairy Godmothers to offer their gifts, the

young Fairy quickly rose from her chair and stepped behind the tapestry near the baby's cradle, so that she might be the last to speak. In this way she hoped to undo – as far as she could – the evil that the offended Godmother might plan.

The Fairies began to bestow their gifts on the Princess. The first said Aurora should be the most beautiful girl in the world; the second, that Aurora should say things wittily; the third, that Aurora should be graceful in every movement. The fourth Fairy promised that Aurora should dance as lightly as a feather; the fifth, that Aurora should out-sing the nightingale; and the sixth, that Aurora should play exquisitely on all kinds of musical instruments. Now that it was the turn of the Oldest Fairy, she hobbled forward with her staff, and bending over the cradle she said, as she trembled with rage, "*I* promise you, Princess Aurora, that you shall run the sharp point of a spindle into your hand – and you will *die*!"

When the company heard this frightful curse, they were aghast. Some wept. The Queen fainted. The King grew pale. Just at this moment the young Fairy came from behind the tapestry to make her gift, the final one.

"Your Majesties, be comforted!" she said. "Your

daughter will *not* die by this prophesy. I cannot undo entirely what the powerful Oldest Fairy has decreed, but her curse shall be softened. The Princess will pierce her hand with a spindle, it is true, but instead of dying she will fall into a deep, deep sleep. After a hundred years, a king's son will come to wake her to a happy life."

The guests were hardly gone before the King issued an order that every single spindle in his kingdom must be broken at once, and burned. No one could own or use a spindle in spinning, nor even have one in the house, on pain of death. The King meant to protect his little Princess.

One day, exactly sixteen years later, when the King and Queen were away at another of their estates, the young Princess was playing at exploring the castle. Climbing from room to room until she reached the top of one of the towers, she was drawn by the sound of a spinning wheel. Here in a cramped little attic nook, a pleasant old granny sat drawing the yarn off the wheel and winding it onto her spindle, as she had done for years. She had never even heard of the King's edict against spindles.

"What are you doing, Granny?" asked the Princess. "What are you making?"

"I'm spinning, and I'm making yarn, dearie," replied the old woman, not knowing she spoke to a Princess.

"What a pretty pastime!" exclaimed Princess Aurora. "Do let me see if *I* can do it."

But she had no more than taken up the stick and given the wheel a start, than she ran the sharp point of the wooden spindle into her hand, just as the Fairy had said she was to do. The Princess immediately sank to the floor in a faint.

The old woman, shocked and terrified, began to call down the steps with all her might. "Help, help!" People from all over the castle ran up, up, up the stairs, two at a time. They threw water on the face of the Princess; they loosened her clothing; they tried to warm her hands with rubbing; they patted cologne on her forehead – but nothing could rouse her.

There was so much noise that the King, who had just returned to the castle, came dashing up the stairs to see what was the matter. Recalling what the two Fairies had said so long ago, he realized sadly that he had not been able to avoid what was prophesied. He blamed no one, certainly not the poor old granny.

He carried the young Princess tenderly to the best room in the castle and placed her on a bed. She was so beautiful, she looked like an angel. In her swoon, her cheeks had not lost their color and her lips were as red as coral. Though her eyes were closed, the sound of her gentle breathing showed that she was not dead. The King ordered that she should be left to sleep in peace, until the hour of her awakening should come.

At the time the spindle pierced the Princess, the good Fairy who had saved her life by changing the Oldest Fairy's curse, happened to be twelve thousand leagues away, in the Kingdom of Mataquin. But just the same, the news was brought to her at once, by a little dwarf with seven-league boots (that is, boots which take the wearer across seven leagues at a stride). She promptly set out in her carriage of fire, drawn by seven dragons.

She was at the Palace within the hour. The King came out to greet her, and helped her down from the chariot.

The good Fairy Godmother approved of everything he had done. But, foresighted as she was, she realized that when the time came for the Princess to open her eyes, Aurora would be most upset to find she was all by herself in the big old castle.

So this is what she did. With her wand she touched everyone in the castle – except the King and the Queen. She touched the governesses, the ladies-in-waiting, the chambermaids, the gentlemen, the officers of the household, the butlers, the cooks, the kitchen boys, the couriers, the watchmen, the Swiss Guards, the pages and the footmen.

She also touched the horses in the stables and their grooms, the great mastiffs in the courtyard, and even little Puff, the Princess's dog, who lay in his basket.

As the Fairy Godmother went about her magic with her wand, she kept saying softly, "You shall close your eyes and sleep; you shall sleep until the Princess is awakened. Sleep well, have happy dreams."

The moment she touched them, they all fell asleep as deeply as the Princess, stopping short in the midst of whatever they were doing. Even the spits turning above the fire, roasting a row of partridges and pheasants, fell asleep; and the fire slept, too.

All this was done in a twinkling, for fairies are very quick at their work.

Having kissed their beloved child, who slept quietly on, the King and the Queen went to sit on their thrones, and then the Fairy put them into the enchanted sleep. They had meant to issue proclamations forbidding anyone to come near. But these proclamations were unnecessary, for within a quarter of an hour a vast number of trees, great and small, had grown up around the park; sprinkled among them were briars and thorny bushes, so closely interlaced that neither man nor beast could get through them. Even from a distance you could see nothing of the castle except the tips of the towers.

Without question the Fairy had left no stone unturned, to make sure that while she slept, the Princess would be guarded from inquisitive eyes.

A century later, the son of a king from a far country was out hunting in that part of the country where the sleeping kingdom lay. He asked his guides what towers were those which he could see above the tangled brambles, and everyone told him a different story! Some said that it was an old castle haunted by ghosts; others said that all the witches far and near held their sabbaths there. The story most people believed was that it was the retreat of an ogre who nightly prowled about and carried off all the children he could catch to eat. There he would eat them at his leisure, since no one could follow him, as only the ogre knew how to pass through the fierce brambles.

The Prince was puzzled about what to believe, until finally an old, old peasant spoke up and said, "Your Highness, more than fifty years ago, I heard my father tell that there was a beautiful Princess in the castle – more beautiful than any other Princess in the whole world! There she slumbers, and must go on slumbering, a hundred years. Then, it is said, she will be wakened by the son of a king, for whom she is destined."

At these words, the young Prince felt his heart on fire. He had no doubts that *he* was the one to bring this fine adventure to its end, and, driven by love and the desire for glory, he resolved to find out for himself the truth of this strange and wonderful tale.

No sooner had he reached the wood than all the huge trees, the brambles and the thorn bushes, parted of their own accord to let him through. He strode purposefully toward the castle, which now he could see far down a spacious, tree-lined avenue. Looking back he was astonished to find that none of his retinue had followed him. The trees and brambles and vines had closed together again behind him! However, he went resolutely forward, as young Princes in love are always valiant. He reached the great fore-court, where everything he saw might well have frozen him with fear. The silence was terrifying. The image of death was everywhere. Men and animals lay on the ground as if they were dead. However, he quickly realized from their ruddy faces that the Swiss Guards were only sleeping; empty jugs and a few drops of wine still left in their cups showed that they had been drinking heavily when they fell into slumber.

Stepping over them, the Prince crossed a courtyard paved with marble, and went up the stairs into the Guard Room where the Guards stood nearby ranged in a line, their arquebuses on their shoulders, snoring away noisily.

On and on he walked, through many rooms full of gentlemen and ladies, all asleep, some of them standing up, others sitting down.

At last the Prince reached a gilded door, turned the knob and entered a beautiful chamber paneled in gold and white. There, in bed with scarlet drapes surmounted by a golden crown, lay the most beautiful girl he had ever seen, the lovely young Princess Aurora, who seemed to him to shine with the most radiant and heavenly beauty. In trembling wonder the Prince came closer, and looked upon her sweet face – then bent to kiss her gently.

The spell was now at an end: the Princess wakened, and looked up at him more tenderly than might have seemed proper at a first meeting. "Is that you, my Prince?" she said. "You have kept me waiting a long time."

The Prince was enchanted by her words, and even more by her voice. He did not know how to express his joy and thankfulness. He did not express himself grandly, it is true, but this was no disadvantage, for the less ready the tongue, the greater the love, it is said. He was more at a loss than she was, which is not surprising; she had had plenty of time to dream of what she was going to say to her Prince, since it is very likely – although the story does not mention it – that the Good Fairy had arranged pleasurable dreams for Princess Aurora's sleeping.

They talked and talked, on and on, for four hours, and still had not said even half the things they wanted to say.

Meanwhile, the whole palace had stirred to life at the same moment as the Princess. People started up about their duties, and as they were not all in love, many were dying of hunger. The chief lady-in-waiting, who was as hungry as the others, became impatient, and in a loud voice called at last to the Princess, "Dinner is served."

The Prince gave the Princess his hand and led her into the grand hall to her parents. She was already dressed in magnificent clothes, and since they did not make her any the less beautiful, the Prince was careful not to tell her that her costume was much like one he remembered his grandmother wearing.

They passed into the Hall of Mirrors and dined there, served by the Princess's household. Violins and oboes played old melodies which, although nobody had played them for a hundred years, were still excellent. After dinner, with the joyful consent of the King and Queen, the Prince and Aurora were married that day by the Grand Almoner in the castle chapel. And legend has it that they lived happily ever after.

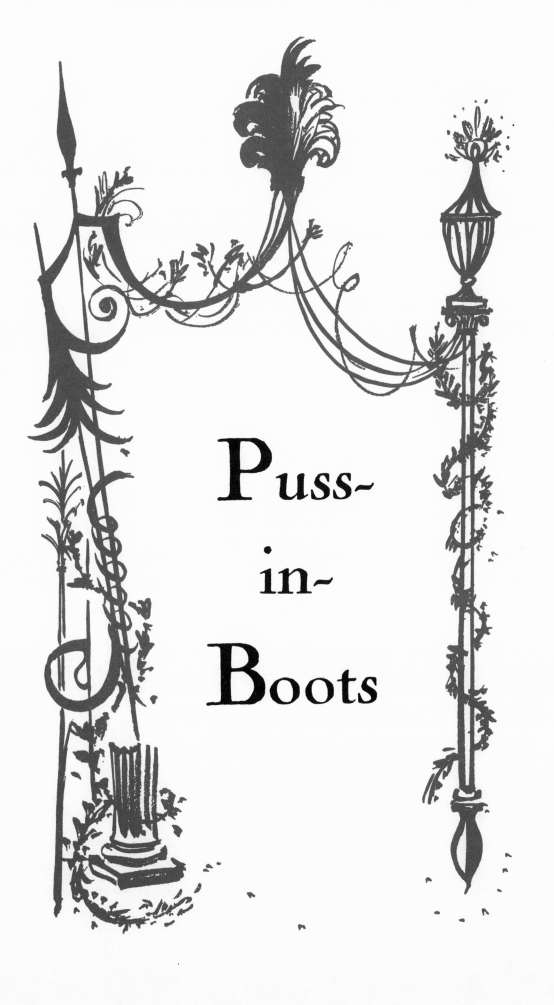

Puss-
-in-
Boots

Puss-in-Boots

THERE was once a poor miller who at his death had nothing to leave his three sons but a small flour mill, a Donkey, and a black-and-white Cat.

This modest estate was all too easy to divide among the sons. They decided not to call in a lawyer, who, they felt, would only mix them up with "thereas" and "hereinafter" and "inasmuchas", and then, like as not, end by owning everything himself. So the eldest son took the flour mill, the second son took the Donkey, and the youngest son was left with only the black-and-white Cat.

The youngest son felt bleak at the thought of his disappointing inheritance. He said to himself, "My brothers can earn a decent living by joining forces. The mill and the Donkey naturally work together. But what am *I* going to do? All I have is an extra burden, another mouth to feed. Of course," and he smiled wryly, "I might *eat* the Cat – and make a pair of gloves out of his fur. Then what?"

He remembered a little joke his father used to recite when his boys bothered him to give them a reason for something. They would ask, "What *for*, Papa? What *for*?" "What *fer*? *Cat* fur," he would answer. "Cat fur to make kitten-breeches." Now the son could indeed make kitten-breeches out of Papa's tomcat.

But that would be a mean jest, with no sense to it.

He sighed and finally said to himself, "There's nothing left for me to do but lie down and die of hunger. I have absolutely no prospects."

The black-and-white Cat had heard every word his young owner said, though he politely pretended not to have been listening.

"Don't be too upset, Master mine," he suddenly spoke up. "You have forgotten that I am a *money-cat*, with extra toes. Observe!" And the black-and-white Cat stretched out his paws for his young master to see. Sure enough, there were the extra toes that so many considered to be very lucky in a cat.

"Now, Master dear, stop worrying," the Cat continued. "Just get me a tow-sack and a fistful of cabbage leaves. And have a pair of boots made for me – on credit, *of course* – so I can go through the briar patch. You may find that your father's tomcat isn't such a bad legacy, after all!"

The Cat's remarks cheered his master a little. He was inclined to believe him, for he had seen the Cat do some truly clever tricks. For instance, Puss would hide in a flour bin to ambush a rat. Or he would drape himself over the edge of an empty barrel on its side, his front legs and half his body dangling limp as a rag, as if he had drawn his last breath. Then when along came a couple of mice – unafraid of the dead cat – down he would drop, quick as a flash. He was a mighty hunter, the young man knew. So the Cat's proposal struck him as at least worth a try, especially as he had no better plan of his own.

As soon as the Cat had what he had asked for, he pulled on the boots, flung the tow-sack with the cabbage leaves inside, over his shoulder, and grabbed the drawstrings in his oversized front paws. Then away he went to the briar patch, where he found a good spot, put down the sack, rolled back the mouth of the sack, and arranged the cabbage leaves in artful carelessness.

Then he lay down on the ground, beside the sack, stiff as if he were dead. It would not be too long, he was sure, before some gullible young rabbit, unsuspecting the snares of this world, would think he saw a fine free lunch and hop in to get the greens.

He had no more than settled himself than his trick worked. A giddy young rabbit, too silly to live, came hopping by, saw the cabbage leaves and jumped right into the open sack. Before he ever knew what happened to him, Puss-in-Boots (as his master called him when he put on his little footgear) had twisted

26

together the neck of the sack and then strangled the stupidly trusting rabbit.

But instead of taking his quarry home, the Cat went straight to the palace and asked to be admitted to the King. His air was so proud and assured that no one questioned him, but led him directly to His Majesty, before whom Puss made a deep bow.

"Sire," he said, "I present to you a thoroughbred tender rabbit for your Majesty's table. It is a gift from the warren of my master, the Marquis of Carabas." Puss-in-Boots had made up the fancy name for the miller's impoverished son, on the spur of the moment.

"Thank your master for his kindness," replied the King, "and say that his gift gives us pleasure."

Another day, the Cat hid in a cornfield and with a bit of grain (which he had borrowed from the miller's flour mill) cunningly scattered inside his open tow-sack, caught two plump partridges. These he took at once to the King, just as he had taken the rabbit, and presented them as gifts from the Marquis of Carabas. Since everyone loves a present, even those in high places, the King felt flattered and pleased. He gave the Cat a little red velvet pouch filled with bright coins.

Puss-in-Boots carried this little surprise to his

young master, who was delighted. "I *told* you to remember that I'm a money-cat," said Puss. But he made no further explanation of how he came by the gold coins, though the miller's son was immensely curious.

For two or three months, the Cat followed this routine of catching small game and bringing it to the King as gifts from the hunting preserves of his master, the Marquis of Carabas. One day he heard that the King was to take a drive along the riverside with his daughter, the loveliest Princess in the world. Puss-in-Boots lost no time in returning to his young master, and saying, "If you will just do exactly what I am about to suggest, your fortune is made. All you have to do is to bathe in the river at the place I'll show you – and leave the rest to me."

The Marquis of Carabas followed the instructions of the Cat, although he had not the faintest notion of what good could come of this river bathing. While he splashed away, the King's carriage approached, and suddenly as it was very near, the Cat began to bawl loudly, "Help! Help! the high and mighty Marquis of Carabas is drowning!"

The King stuck his head out of the carriage window, and recognizing the Cat who had so often brought

him presents from the famous Marquis, he ordered
his footmen to run and save the drowning man.

As the startled Marquis was being hauled out of
the river, his aide, the Cat, stepped up to the carriage
for a word with His Majesty. "Sire, I fear that my
master cannot come forward to give you proper
thanks, particularly as you have the charming lady,
your daughter, with you. The truth is that he was set
upon by robbers, who took all his gold and his fine
clothes and murderously threw him into the water.
I tried to stop them – you may have heard me shout
'Stop thief' – but it was no use." (The truth was quite
different, of course, for that clever rascal, Puss-in-
Boots, had stuffed his master's shabby clothes under
a big stone).

The King, himself of trim figure not too unlike that
of the Marquis (who had by now retreated to a shoulder-
deep spot in the river) quickly dispatched his Gentleman
of the Wardrobe to the Castle. "Bring back my best
carmine or emerald velvet suit for the Marquis of
Carabas," he commanded. The King felt kindly toward
this young man whom he had rescued.

Once the young man had dressed in the rich royal
costume which was brought to him, he really looked
as if he must be a Marquis. The Princess, seeing how

handsome and nice he was, found him most attractive. Before he had more than looked at her twice – and with respectful though interested glances – she fell completely in love with him.

The King insisted on his getting into the carriage and continuing their ride with them. The resourceful Cat, delighted with the way things were turning out, ran ahead until he came to a meadow where mowers worked. "Mowers and wielders of scythes!" he saluted them: "Hear this message. When the King comes along in a few minutes and asks whose field this is that's being mowed, you say it belongs to the Marquis of Carabas. If you don't, you'll all be chopped up into mincemeat!"

When the King's carriage paused a few minutes later, and the King, sure enough, looked out to ask whose meadow was being mowed, the mowers, still shaken by the Cat's threat, answered in chorus, "It belongs to the Marquis of Carabas!"

"That's a fine property you have there," said the King to the Marquis.

"Yes, Sire, it's not too bad. Quite a nice yield every year. Not bad," replied the Marquis, "not bad at all."

Puss-in-Boots, darting on ahead of the carriage, came up to a band of harvesters reaping grain. He stopped and addressed them: "Reapers! Listen to my message. When the King rides by here in a few minutes and asks whose grain is being harvested, you say it belongs to the Marquis of Carabas. If you don't, you'll all be chopped into mincemeat." And away went the Cat.

When the King's carriage paused a few minutes later, and the King looked out to ask whose crop was being harvested, the reapers answered with one voice, "It belongs to the Marquis of Carabas."

"Think of that!" exclaimed the King. "You do very well, young man! Hayfields, and grain farms – and pastures, too, I have no doubt. Orchards, perhaps? And I am not forgetting your game preserves, from which your emissary the Cat-with-boots has brought me many gifts for the royal table."

The young man, warming to his new identity as a modest rich man, nodded in matter-of-course agreement with the King, and smiled – not too boldly – at the Princess. As the drive continued, the carriage made more stops at pastures and orchards (as the King had guessed) where the field hands, to a man, always said what Puss-in-Boots had warned them to say: "These lands belong to the Marquis of Carabas!"

The Cat, continuing to run in advance of the royal

coach, came at last to an imposing castle, built in the Italian mode, its roof made of red tile which could be seen long before one reached the portal. The master of this fine castle – and owner of all those fields and meadows to which the Cat had laid claim for the Marquis of Carabas – was a powerful ogre. The Cat quickly found out about him from a gardener. There seemed to be a hustle and bustle about the grounds, in preparation for a feast of some sort. Puss-in-Boots seized the opportunity to catch the sleeve of a servant and send in a message to the ogre. "Tell your master that a famous traveler has heard of his wonderful talents, and cannot think of passing by the castle without greeting and paying his respects to one so highly regarded."

The Ogre received his visitor as cordially as it is in the nature of an ogre to do, and invited him to sit down and rest for a bit. "I am about to have a little party. Perhaps you will stay?"

Puss-in-Boots bowed and said thank you. "My real hope was – dear Sire - not to impose upon your kindness but rather to ask about your magical powers of changing your shape. I hear that you can become any sort of animal you please. Is this remarkable story true? My informant had not actually *seen* you

change into an elephant or a lion, but he insisted that you *really* could do it."

The Ogre, annoyed by the tone of disbelief in the Cat's question, snapped, "You don't think it's so? Well, just watch me turn into a lion!" And the next instant, where the Ogre had been, a tawny lion shook himself and reached out a paw toward Puss-in-Boots.

The Cat, utterly taken by surprise and fright, ran up to the roof, and then slid and slipped and skittered down into the rain-gutter, because his little boots could get no hold on the tiles. His whiskers trembled. He began to think he had made a bad mistake in coming into this castle, when suddenly he saw that the Ogre had gone back to his natural shape. The Cat slid down by way of a drain pipe, and said admiringly to his host: "You gave me a turn there, for a minute. Somehow, I hadn't realized you could act so fast. You do these *big* transformations well ... But I am wondering how good you are with the truly difficult ones – the *small* animals. A wizard friend of mine, who does this sort of thing, says turning into a lion is almost no trick at all, but that turning into a rat, or harder yet, a mouse, is next to impossible!"

"Impossible?" roared the Ogre, his vanity touched. "For me, *nothing* is impossible." And there he was, a tiny mouse on the floor, scowling at the Cat as no mouse ever had dared before. As soon as the Cat saw this change in the Ogre, he jumped and with one swipe of his oversized paws broke the neck of the mouse and devoured him.

Then he said to the Chief Butler, "Tell the servants they have a new master – the Marquis of Carabas. The party you are preparing is for the Marquis, who will be here soon in the company of the King and his daughter, the Princess. The Ogre left hurriedly, bidding me to give you his message."

By this time, the King's carriage had reached the castle gates. The King assumed, rightly of course, that he had come to the dwelling of the owner of the fields and meadows, and thought he had brought the young Marquis to the door of his home. The Marquis, quaking inside, could not imagine what he would do, now that his pretense was about to be unmasked.

Just then, Puss-in-Boots appeared, and with a sweeping bow, he said, "Welcome, your Majesty and your Highness the Princess, to the country lodge of the Marquis of Carabas!"

The King, whose pleasure was matched by the surprise of the Marquis (who wisely held his tongue), exclaimed, "So this is your castle? Splendid! The courtyard and the surrounding buildings are impressive. Let's see the beauty of the inside."

The Marquis gave his hand to the lovely Princess, and together they followed the King into the castle and the great hall, where the Ogre's table was set for a feast. Puss-in-Boots waved his paw to summon the Chief Butler, and immediately a whole procession of delicious viands came in on silver trays. This hospitality and the rich trappings of the castle and six glasses of good wine prompted the King to suggest to the Marquis, "You have only to say the words that your eyes have spoken to my daughter, Mirabel, here, and I think she will answer *yes*. For my part, I am glad to have you for a son-in-law!"

The Marquis looked tenderly at the Princess, who gave him a smile of consent, and with no more ado this charming pair were married before nightfall.

The Cat, much loved by the Marquis, was made a great lord. He pulled off his boots for good and all, for they cramped his hind feet; he made a point always of lying only on his master's dark blue suits (so his white hairs would shed and show on it) and the Princess' white shawl (in order that he could leave his black hairs there), and he gave up game hunting, except to catch an occasional overbold mouse.

Blue
Beard

Blue Beard

ONCE upon a time there was a fabulously rich man who owned magnificent houses both in town and in the country. He had silver and gold plate made especially for his table. His furniture was upholstered with fine silk brocade with his coat of arms. Horses in matched pairs drew his gilded carriages. His carpets were imported from Persia, his coverlets were woven in the Vale of Kashmir, and he had puffed-up embroidered ottomans in every corner.

Unfortunately a blue beard grew from his chin. This made him look so grim and terrifying that every

woman or girl who saw him turned and ran.

One of his neighbors, a lady of quality, had two sons and two extraordinarily beautiful daughters. He asked for the hand of one of these girls in marriage, but as both charmed him – he said – he could not make up his mind which he wanted the more. So he asked their mother to choose between them for him.

The difficulty was that neither girl wished to marry him, not liking the idea of a husband with a blue beard, no matter how wealthy he might be. Each tried to palm him off on the other.

The elder sister, Anne, said, "Prudence, *you* can have him."

But Prudence declined the offer. "Oh, no, Sister Anne! You're the elder. *You* should be the first to marry. Take him yourself, and I'll dance at your wedding."

What made them shy away from the idea still more than the blue beard was the fact that the man had already been married a number of times, and nobody quite knew what had become of his other wives.

With an idea that perhaps it would help if they were all to get better acquainted, Blue Beard invited the two sisters, their two brothers and their mother, along with a number of young friends, to come and spend a gala week at one of his country estates.

The time was agreeably filled in many pleasurable ways. The host offered his stables of thoroughbred horses to the guests, and they all went riding and hunting in his wooded acres. They fished in Blue Beard's lake, where the silver trout so abounded that it was impossible not to catch them, and the air rang with little cries of pleasure as the girls drew in their lines. When the gay company were not riding or fishing, they feasted – for Blue Beard's cooks roasted the tenderest meats, baked the tallest cakes and served the finest wines to be had.

When the guests were not feasting, they danced. When they were not dancing, they sang, or they played charades. To Blue Beard, who had passed his first youth some time ago, this toying and teasing and staying up all the night might have been tiring. But if it was, he gave no sign, made no complaint. The game was worth the candle, because at the end he would surely win one of the two lovely sisters as his wife.

The week-long party was so much fun that the younger girl, Prudence, began to look at the host with a favorable eye. "I don't know that his beard is so blue, after all," she said to her mother. "And what if it *is?* What's *wrong* with a blue beard? It's really rather interesting, come to think of it, and not at all common – like brown or black."

"You're very right, Prudence, dear," agreed her mother, who wanted to have this rich man in the family, anyhow. "And, also, even a blue beard will turn white eventually."

So, having persuaded herself, the younger sister let her suitor know she had chosen him, and when they returned to town she married him.

A month later, Blue Beard told his wife that he had to go away on important business for some six weeks. "Don't be lonesome while I am traveling," he told her. "Invite some of your friends to come and stay with you, and enjoy yourself. You can all go to the country if you like, and don't stint on entertaining, wife. Be lavish."

Then he handed her a metal hoop strung with keys. He explained, "Here are the keys of the two large storerooms. These next keys are for the special gold

and silver table services that we don't use every day. These keys fit the strongboxes where I keep my money, coins in gold and silver. These open my chests of jewels. And this one is the masterkey to all the rooms." He paused and looked at her sharply, holding out a small key. "*This* little one you had better put aside, because you are *not* to use it," he added meaningly.

"It unlocks the closet at the end of the long gallery on the ground floor. I don't care what else in the house you open or explore. But *forget* about that little room. I forbid you to look into it. If you disobey me, even for the smallest minute, and unlock that closet door, I will know it and you will rue the day."

Prudence promised to carry out his instructions faithfully. Blue Beard embraced her, entered his carriage, and set off on his journey.

Her close friends and neighbors did not wait on ceremony before flocking over to call on the young bride. They were impatient to see all the splendors of her house, most of them not having dared to come and visit when her husband was at home, because they felt terrified of his blue beard. Now they came hurrying and crowding in, bustling through the rooms as if they were at an auction sale and must examine

every rich thing before someone snatched it away. They looked into the wardrobes, fingering the rich clothes. They pulled open drawers, rummaging freely. They climbed up to the storerooms where the quantities of elegant tapestries and embroidered linens, the beds, the sofas, the inlaid chests and fruitwood tables made their jaws drop.

They touched the silk curtains, and marveled at the glass cabinets of ivory trinkets. And they smiled at their own images reflected in the full-length mirrors. What frames of crystal, silver and gilt enamel, more exquisite than any they had seen! The visitors kept saying how lucky their friend was, and how they envied her good fortune.

But Prudence, who had already seen most of her husband's dazzling possessions, had her mind on the room she had *not* seen, and was not supposed to see. At last she was so overcome with curiosity that, not stopping to think how rude it was to desert her visitors, she hurried down the small back staircase so quickly that two or three times she thought she might trip and break her neck.

When she reached the door to the closet, she recalled her husband's orders. "Well," she thought rebelliously, "if he *really* did not want me to unlock

the door, why did he leave the key with me? Wouldn't it have been easier for him to have kept it in his own pocket and say nothing?" Handing her the key, Prudence finally decided, amounted almost to *telling* her to look at the one plain little room she might otherwise neglect. Yes – she *must* open it!

She hesitated a moment, reflecting on what might happen if she disobeyed Blue Beard. But how could he know?

The temptation was too great. So she took the little key, thrust it into the keyhole, and turned it. Then, with trembling hands, she opened the door of the closet. At first she could not see a thing, because the shutters were closed. After a little while, as her eyes grew accustomed to the light filtering through the slats of each shutter, Prudence stared at the bare wooden floor. What made it such a strange red-brown color, in great spread-out patches? It looked for all the world like pools of – yes – *blood*, dried on the floor!

As a cold terror crept through her veins, Prudence raised her eyes to perceive the body of a woman – Blue Beard's wife? – hanging from the wall. And beside her, another woman – another wife? – her dress stained in a long stream from the slash in her poor neck. Beyond her hung another victim and yet an-

50

other – until Prudence counted seven, all hanging like coats in a cloakroom.

These were the wives Blue Beard had married, and whose throats he had cut one after the other!

She thought she would die of fear, and she shook so that the key of the closet, which she had taken out of the lock, dropped from her nerveless hand. When she had come to herself a bit, she picked up the little key, backed out of the room, shut and locked the door, and sped back to her guests. They had not missed her, for her well-trained servants had been offering refreshments. But as soon as the company said their good-byes and the last straggler had left, Prudence retired to her bedroom to think upon her frightful discovery.

Suddenly she noticed that the little key, which she had tucked away in her pocket, bore a dark stain. She tried to wipe it clean with the ruffle of her petticoat. The blood would not come off. Frantically she ran for water, and washed the key, but her efforts were in vain. She rubbed soap on the metal without effect, and then scrubbed it fiercely with a pumice stone.

But the blood that the key had touched when it fell to the floor of Blue Beard's closet could not be rubbed away, not even when in desperation the young wife took a file and scraped at it with all her might. This was a magic key, and if she was able to remove the blood from one side, it immediately showed up on the other. Poor Prudence did not know what she was going to do!

That very evening Blue Beard came home from his journey. He told his wife that while he was on the road, a messenger had caught up with him to bring word that the business which had needed his attention had been settled, to his advantage, so that he need go no further. Prudence nodded and asked him how he felt and told him her friends had all admired the fine house. She pretended to be delighted at her husband's return, but her heart beat with fear.

The next day Blue Beard asked her for the hoop of keys and she gave them to him. Her hand shook so badly that he guessed at once what had happened. But first he checked through the keys she had given back to him.

"Um-mm, the key for the large storerooms of furniture, I see here. And for the chests of gold and silver table services. Good, good. And this pair for my money chests – you examined the gold coins, I suppose, dear wife? Some of them go back to Roman times. Ah-h-h, *this* key opens the jewel caskets. You liked the trays of diamonds and sea-green emeralds, I suppose? And perhaps we might have a rope of pigeon-blood rubies to go around your pretty little neck?" He laughed, not too pleasantly.

"And here is the master-key to *all* the rooms." As he swung this final key down along the hoop to join the others, he looked sharply at Prudence, who avoided his eye. "Now where is my little closet key, the one you did *not* use?" Prudence trembled until she could hardly speak, yet she managed to say, "Oh, I must have left it upstairs on my dressing table."

"Be sure to let me have it soon," said Blue Beard.

His wife made an excuse for not finding it, the next day, and the next – but at last she could not put it off any longer. She handed Blue Beard the key.

He turned it over and over in his hand.

"Why is there blood on this key?" he demanded.

"I don't know," whispered his poor wife, paler than death.

"You don't know?" mocked Blue Beard. "Well, *I* know! Very well, Madam, into that closet *you* shall go and take your place among the ladies you saw there!"

Prudence threw herself at her husband's feet, weeping and asking her forgiveness.

"Dear husband, I love you, and I am sorry to have

done what displeased you. Forgive me, and let me show you how faithfully I can follow all your wishes," she pleaded.

Her beauty and her penitence would have moved a stone, but Blue Beard's heart was hard as flint. He had made up his mind.

"You must die, Madam," he said coldly, "and at once!"

"If I have to die," she replied, looking at him through a flood of tears, "give me at least a little time to say my prayers."

"You may have ten minutes, and not a minute more," said Blue Beard.

As she walked away, thinking to go into the garden, she met her sister Anne, coming into the house for a day's visit. Her sister meant to keep the young wife company, for she supposed Blue Beard still to be away on his business errand.

In the same instant that her sister asked what made her look so wild, Prudence cried to her, "Heaven has sent you! Are our brothers with you? My husband means to kill me – in nine minutes from now!"

"Yes, yes," her alarmed sister cried, "our brothers are on their way, but they had to stop because one of their horses cast a shoe. Let me run to the tower window and look out for them!"

"Go – go up to the parapet and see if they are coming along the road, Sister Anne. They promised that they would visit with me today, but if they do not come soon, it will be too late!"

She waited barely long enough for her sister to reach the parapet before calling up to her, "Sister Anne, Sister Anne, what do you see?"

And Sister Anne answered, "I see nothing but the green grass growing, and the dust floating in the sun."

By this time, Blue Beard, making a few slashes through the air with his heavy saber, shouted to his wife, "Come down! Your time is up! Come down at once."

"I'm coming, I'm coming!" she answered him. More softly, she called up to the tower, "Sister Anne, Sister Anne, do you see anyone coming?"

"Oh, no! All I see is the green grass growing and dust floating in the sun."

"Come down this very moment or I shall come up after you!" bellowed angry Blue Beard.

"Give me time to write one line to my mother," the young wife called piteously. And then again she asked the tower watcher, "Sister Anne, Sister Anne, do you see anyone coming?"

"I see a big cloud of dust headed this way."

"Is it our brothers?"

"Alas, no, dear Prudence. It is a flock of sheep!"

"Are you coming down," roared Blue Beard, "or must I *drag* you down?"

"Just one tiny second, husband mine! I am saying farewell to my dearest mother."

Then to her sister she called once more: "Sister Anne, Sister Anne, what do you see now?"

"I see two horsemen galloping toward us. But they are far off. Heaven be praised! It is our brothers! I am waving my scarf to signal them to hurry."

By this time, Blue Beard, outraged at the delay, came to the bottom of the stairs and shouted so that the walls shook, and his wife crept trembling down the carpeted steps. As she reached the end of her slow descent, Blue Beard seized her wrist and flung her to the floor.

"Spare me! Spare me! Just one more moment!" Prudence begged. She hoped to spin out the time a little, and by distracting Blue Beard to give her brothers a chance to come closer.

But Blue Beard had no intention of waiting any longer to finish off his victim. He seized her by her hair and said, "Now make your last prayers!" Then

he raised his saber to strike off her head.

At that moment there was a loud clamor and thundering at the gate, so insistent that Blue Beard stopped short. The gate flew open and in came the two horsemen, who leaped off their mounts and ran at Blue Beard with their swords bared. He recognized the brothers of his wife, and flinging her aside, he dashed away to escape. But as poor Prudence fainted, the two brothers pursued her wicked husband, and ran him through with their swords. They left him as dead as his seven wives.

Poor Prudence opened her eyes when her brothers returned to her, but had not the strength to rise and embrace them or her Sister Anne who had come down with all speed from the top of the tower.

It turned out that Blue Beard had no heirs, so his wife became mistress of his vast estates. She used a part of her wealth to marry her Sister Anne to a young man who had been in love with her for years.

Another part went to buy Captains' commissions for her two brothers. The rest was her own portion when she herself married a really fine and agreeable man who helped her to forget the harrowing time she had had with Blue Beard.

Hop
'
o my
Thumb

Hop o' my Thumb

THERE once lived a woodcutter and his wife who had seven children, all boys. The oldest was ten, and the youngest was seven. It may seem curious that the woodcutter should have had so large a family in so short a while, but his wife believed in doing things quickly, so she never had less than two at a time, except for the last little boy. This made three sets of twins and one little boy – so small and puny that the other children and the parents considered him the runt.

When he was born, this littlest one, he was no

larger than your thumb, so they called him *Hop o'my Thumb*. Because he grew slowly and never had much to say, they mistook his quietness for stupidity. Yet the truth was that Hop o'my Thumb had better sense and judgment than all his six older brothers put together. He noticed and understood what went on around him. That is why, when he saw that day after day there was less and less food on the table to eat – until at last only one dry and twisted yellow turnip was left to be cooked – he wondered what would happen.

On that evening, after the children were in bed, with their knitted caps pulled down over their ears to keep them warm, the woodcutter and his wife sat by the fire, sadly. The woodcutter finally spoke desperately to his wife.

"We cannot feed the children any longer. This is the worst famine I have ever known, and the end is not in sight. I can't bear to see the boys waste away and starve before our eyes, so I've decided that tomorrow I shall take them into the woods and lose them. It will not be hard, because while they are busy tying up faggots, you and I can slip away without their noticing."

"Oh, no, no, NO!" cried the wife. "You *can't* do

that! How can you even think of taking your own children out and losing them?"

The woodcutter reasoned with his distracted wife.

"Alas, my dear, what else can we do? Except for that withered turnip, we have no morsel of food for our children or ourselves."

"It makes no difference," sobbed the mother. "I can't agree to this cruel plan. I am poor, but I am their mother!"

Long into the night the two parents talked, with Hop o'my Thumb listening. When finally, and sorrowfully, the mother and father agreed they could not watch their children starve, and went to bed, Hop o'my Thumb stayed awake, thinking.

Early next morning he slipped out and went to the brookside, where he filled his pockets with little white pebbles before returning home. The woodcutter lined up his three sets of twins, with Hop o'my Thumb at the end, and calling his wife to come along, set forth for the middle of the forest. Hop o'my Thumb said nothing to his brothers about what he knew. As he walked, he dropped the white pebbles onto the ground.

They came at length to a part of the forest so dense that they could not see each other ten paces away.

Here the woodcutter began to chop wood, and the little boys tied branches into bundles, to make a fire. As soon as the parents saw that the children were too busy tying twigs to notice, the mother and father quickly drew away, then with longer and longer steps hastened down a sidepath and out of the woods.

When the boys saw they were left alone, they began to cry and call for their parents. They did not know which way to return, and became more frightened each moment. But Hop o'my Thumb calmed them.

"Don't be afraid, brothers," he said. "I knew this was going to happen, and I'll get you home safely, if you just follow me."

So he led the six of them along the trail he had marked with the white pebbles, right to the door of their own cottage. There they stopped, outside, not quite daring to go in, yet trying to hear through the door what their mother and father were saying.

Now it happened that at the very time the parents had returned, a servant had come from the lord of the manor house nearby to deliver a side of venison.

Said he, "Milord had good success at hunting today, and since he knows you have seven children to feed in this dreadful famine, he sends you this meat as a present."

As he left, the woodcutter's wife burst into tears.

"What good is meat when those we would give it to are not here to share it? Oh, where are our poor children? It was *your* idea, William, to lose them! I told you it was wrong. By now the wolves may have eaten them, and it's all your fault. You were cruel and wicked to abandon our children. Oh, where are my little boys now? Where *are* they?"

She called out so loudly that her children heard her through the door. They all shouted together happily, "*Here* we are, mother! *Here* we are!" Whereupon their mother flung open the door and she and the father hugged the children joyfully.

As their mother prepared the bountiful supper, the boys told over and over what a terrible time they had had in the forest, all talking at the same time. Then they all ate with great pleasure, rejoicing at being together once more.

But the time again came, not too long thereafter, when there was no more food. In despair, the woodcutter and his wife, feeling that they must really lose the boys now, decided to take them still further into the woods and leave them there, the next day.

Hop o'my Thumb overheard this, and he resolved to do as he had done before. But when he crept from bed in the early morning hours to slip out and gather his white pebbles at the brookside, the doors of the cottage had been bolted tight, and he could not open them.

There was nothing Hop o'my Thumb could do. He worried until, as all the brothers were lined up for walk into the woods, the mother gave each child a piece of bread – the last bread she had. As his brothers munched theirs, Hop o'my Thumb did not eat his piece, but shoved it into his pocket. Then he secretly pinched off little bits and dropped them along the way as he had previously dropped the white pebbles.

When, later, the parents stole away from the children in the thickest part of the forest, Hop o'my Thumb had no fear. He was sure that all he had to do was to lead his brothers where he had marked the road with crumbs. To his dismay, however, he could not find a single pinch of the bread. Birds had come and eaten every bit!

The children wandered in circles, getting more lost the further they walked. Dark came on, a howling wind began to blow, and the little boys thought they heard wolves closing in to eat them. They were scared speechless, hardly daring to look behind them. Then rain poured down, wetting them to the skin.

Miserable and cold, they slipped with each step they took, falling into the mire, getting up muddied from head to foot.

Hop o'my Thumb climbed a tree, to see if he could figure out which way to head next. Looking about in all directions, he spied a little light glimmering like a distant candle far outside the woods. When he came down, the trees hid the light from view, and Hop o'my Thumb could not show it to his brothers. But he led them toward that edge of the forest where he remembered the gleam, and after they had stumbled at his heels for what seemed a long time, they saw it, too.

Summoning strength, the boys kept working their way toward the light. But sometimes when they went down into a hollow, it disappeared and they were afraid they had lost it, until a rise of land brought its flame into view again.

They reached the door at last, and a kind lady opened to their knocking. She asked what they wanted. Hop o'my Thumb spoke for the muddy bedraggled little band of brothers. "We have lost our way," he said. "We are cold, and the wolves may be after us. Could we not come and sleep inside?" Not wanting to ask too much, he added, "You needn't give us anything to eat."

"Needn't give you anything to eat, child? Oh, you poor innocent little ones! Don't you *know* where you are? This is the house of an ogre who eats children and likes nothing better for his supper than little boys. Go away as fast as you can!"

At this dreadful news, the brothers began to cry and to tremble. "We have no place to hide, Madam," said Hop o'my Thumb, shaking and quaking. "If you don't let us come in, the wolves are going to get us tonight! So we might as well stay and be eaten by the ogre gentleman . . . He might even spare us, if you begged him to," he added hopefully.

Moved by pity, the woman took the little boys in, wiped the mud off them, and let them warm themselves near the big roaring fire. On a spit in the fireplace, a whole sheep was roasting for the ogre's supper.

Just as the boys were beginning to feel warm, they heard a loud banging on the door. It was the ogre, returned. Recognizing his knock, his wife quickly lifted the flounce of the bed and motioned for the boys to crawl under and hide. They barely were out of sight when the ogre tramped in and asked if his supper were ready, and the wine drawn. As he sat down to the table and attacked the roast mutton –

still half raw, but all the better to his taste – he paused and sniffed to the left and to the right.

"I smell human flesh," he announced.

"You smell the veal. I've been dressing a tasty calf for tomorrow's dinner," his wife said quickly, to put him off.

"Oh, no. I smell the flesh of children." He glowered at his wife. "There's something odd going on here. What is it?" He rose from his chair and went straight to the bed. Reaching under the flounce, he dragged out the boys, one after another.

"Just as I thought! You tried to cheat me, didn't you, Wife?"

The terrified children – the three sets of twins and Hop o'my Thumb – fell on their knees before their captor and begged for their lives. But the ogre did not listen. He continued to berate the woman. "I'll make you sorry for this trick! Now where is my big knife? I'll carve up these brats, and you can make a sauce for them. I'm expecting three of my ogre friends one day soon, and these tender tidbits will make a delicious treat to offer them." He began to sharpen his knife on a big whetstone, which he held in his left hand.

"What is your hurry?" his wife asked. "Won't you

have plenty of time tomorrow, when you are rested?"

"Stop it! I'll take care of the job now, and the longer they marinate in the sauce, the tenderer they will be."

"But there is so much fresh meat on hand already — all those oxen and sheep and pigs. It's a nuisance, really, to bother with these skinny little things tonight. Hadn't they better be fattened so they're fit to eat?" she suggested.

"You're right, Wife. Give them a good supper and put them to bed."

The ogre's wife was delighted, and gave the children an ample supper. But they were too frightened to eat. As for the ogre, he settled down to his meal, pleased at the fare he would set before his friends. He gulped at least twelve more glasses of wine than he usually drank, so he was giddy when he went to bed.

The wife took the seven little boys up to a room where there were two enormous beds. In one, the seven little daughters of the ogre, each with a crown on her head, lay fast asleep. They looked better asleep, for, awake, they peered at the world from close-set small gray eyes, and the long sharp teeth in their large mouths had already nipped at young babies.

Into the second big bed, the woman put the seven

little boys, each wearing his knitted woolen cap for
warmth. Then, lifting the candle, she went to join
her husband, the ogre.

Hop o'my Thumb lay awake, thinking, while his
brothers slept. The gold crowns of the little ogresses
stuck in his mind and made him think of a plan. So
he quietly slipped from under the cover, which was
easy, because he was the end boy, and, taking the
woolen cap off each of his brothers, Hop o'my Thumb
made an exchange. From the head of each little
ogress he lifted her crown and carefully put on a
woolen cap. On each of his brothers he softly placed
a crown. If the ogre should come in the night and
touch any head, he might mistake the little boys for
his daughters, and the caps on the ogresses might
make the ogre think his own children were the boys.

It turned out just as Hop o'my Thumb had guessed:
in the middle of the night, the ogre woke up and
began to feel sorry he had not followed his first
impulse. He got out of bed, took his great knife, and
groped his way up in the dark to the room where all
the children were sleeping. He came to the boys' bed
and ran his hands over the crowns, touching Hop
o'my Thumb's last of all. The boy scarcely dared
breathe, both from fright for his own life and from

fear that one of his brothers might wake and cry out.

But the ogre was fooled, and he said to himself, "Well! I nearly made a mistake. I must have had too much to drink last night." Then he went to the other bed, where, on his little ogresses, he felt the boys' caps. "Ah, here we are," he said to himself, and with the greatest satisfaction he cut the throats of his own seven offspring. Well pleased and unsuspecting, he went back down to bed.

As soon as Hop o'my Thumb heard the ogre snoring, he woke his brothers and whispered to them to dress as fast as they could and follow him. They silently crept out of the house, through the garden, and away into the forest again, just as it was beginning to be light. They had just met some woodcutters who pointed the way back to their father's house, when the ogre woke up.

He said to his wife, "Go upstairs and dress those little rascals who came in last night." The ogress was surprised at her husband's goodness, not dreaming how he meant the word "dress". She thought he was telling her to put their clothes on them. When she went up and discovered what had befallen the seven little ogresses, she fell in a faint.

The ogre, afraid that his wife would take too long

with the assignment he had given her, tramped up the stairs to help her. When he found her on the floor, and then saw the frightful result of his work in the dark, he let out a terrible roar. "What have I done! Oh, they shall pay for this, those little villains! I'll tear them apart!"

He flung a pitcher of cold water over his wife, and as she came to, he commanded her, "Get me my seven-league boots, quick! I'm going to catch those boys."

His wife brought his boots, and away sped the ogre into the forest. The children saw him as he crashed among the trees, stepping from mountain to mountain, and over rivers and streams in his long boots.

Suddenly the ogre caught sight of the seven little brothers just as they were within a hundred yards of their father's house. Hop o'my Thumb shoved his brothers into a scooped-out place under a boulder close by and then crouched down to watch the ogre.

"Ah, there you are," the ogre shouted, plunging toward the spot where the children had just stood. In his haste and fury, however, he missed his footing as he strode across a valley between them. He fell, rolled downhill, pitched against the boulder and broke his neck.

The little boys crept out and looked fearfully at their erstwhile enemy. Hop o'my Thumb pulled off the ogre's seven-league boots and put them on himself. Big and wide as the boots were, to fit the ogre, astonishingly they immediately shrank to the size of the boy wearing them, for they were magically designed to become large or small, according to the legs of their wearer. They were just right for Hop o'my Thumb.

He took a few long steps and reached the ogre's house, where he told the ogre's wife – who was amazed to see him – "Your husband is in grave danger. He has been caught by a band of robbers who swear to kill him unless he gives them all his gold and silver. He called to me to be his messenger, and made me put on his boots so that I could come here as swiftly as possible, and so you would know I am not an impostor. Give me his valuables, and I'll hurry back."

The good woman, half out of her wits with grief and fright, gathered up everything; there were two sacks full, for the ogre was a good provider even though he had liked to eat little children. Like a flash, Hop o'my Thumb, together with the ogre's wealth, went home to his father's cottage, where he was welcomed with open arms.

Some people say that it isn't true that Hop o'my Thumb robbed the ogre by this trickery. They say that the reason he took the seven-league boots was just to keep the ogre from chasing and catching other little children. And they say they got the facts in the course of their visits and friendship with the woodcutter and his wife. According to these people, when Hop o'my Thumb first put on the magic boots, he went not to the ogre's house but straight to the King. Since he knew the King was concerned about the outcome of a battle that his forces were fighting two hundred miles away, he offered to bring the King news before nightfall.

The King, they say, promised to reward Hop o'my Thumb liberally if he really could bring news. Hop o'my Thumb was as good as his word, and so was the King. And thereafter the King paid his messenger well on many other occasions, until he had acquired enough to return to his father's house.

Whichever way it was, the end proved the same, for Hop o'my Thumb came home with riches enough to keep the family of the woodcutter from ever knowing want, and they all lived happily together ever after.

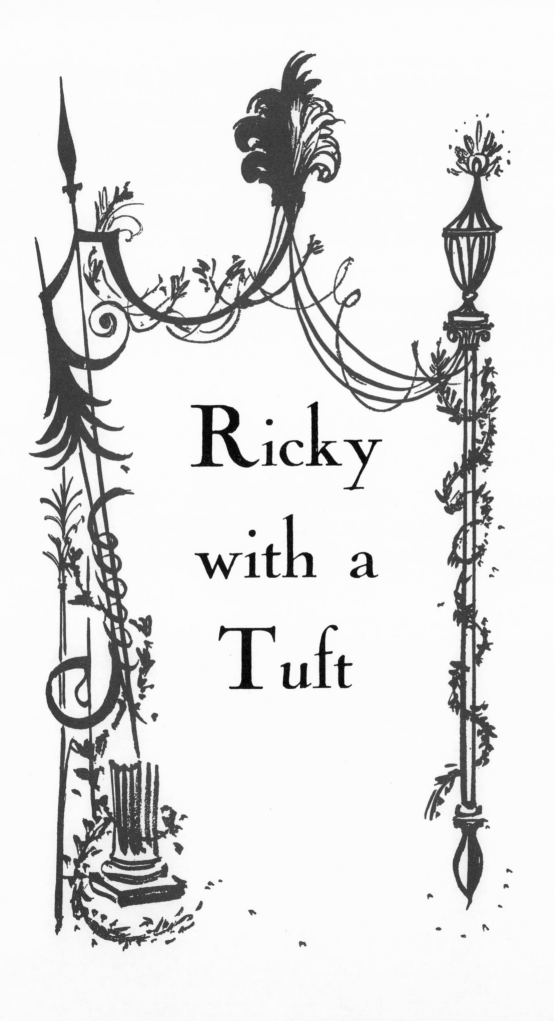

Ricky

with a

Tuft

Ricky with a Tuft

ONCE upon a time there was a Queen who bore a little son so ugly and misshapen that everyone doubted for a time whether he was in fact human. "He's really a gnome," people whispered. "He is a changeling, and later he will turn into another being."

What his mother, the Queen, a sweet lady, had loved about him, when first she held the little fellow in the crook of her arm, was a twist of hair that stuck up on one side of his head. She firmly pressed down this curlicue – this small tuft – with her gentle fingers. But as quickly as she lifted her hand, then up jumped the topknot again! And as often as she tried to flatten this bit of hair it shot right up once more.

The old Nurse who cared for the baby Prince, said, "That's where the cow licked his head. All the best boys have a twist like that. It's a cowlick, that's what."

And instead of Esmond Riquet – his name in the Royal Registry – the odd little Prince came to be called "Cowlicky Ricky," or "Ricky with a Tuft."

Since he seemed such a poor, unlovely child at his birth, his mother's heart was troubled. She feared that except for herself and the King, no one would love this ill-favored little child. However, a Fairy who was present at his birth assured his parents that in spite of the babe's appearance, the child would turn out to be most attractive, since he would be quick-witted and intelligent. She added that she would give him, in addition, the power of bestowing upon the person he loved most in the world, an intelligence equal to his own.

This promise gave a slight comfort to the poor Queen, who had been most upset at bringing so wretched a little monkey into the world, but it by no means succeeded in stilling her misgivings.

Time passed, and Prince Ricky grew older, learned

82

a few words, then began to speak: no sooner had he started to talk than everything he uttered was endearing, and there was something so attractive about all his actions that he charmed everybody.

Seven or eight years later the Queen of a neighboring kingdom bore twin daughters. The first to come into the world was more beautiful than the dawn.

The Queen exclaimed in such delight when she saw her beautiful baby, and clapped her hands over and over again – so ecstatically that her attendants thought her excessive joy might give her a fever! The same Fairy who had been at the birth of little Prince Ricky was also present at the birth of the twins, and to moderate the Queen's rapture she announced that this first little Princess would, alas, be as dim-witted as she was beautiful. The Queen, already cast down by this prophesy, was even more upset when her second daughter, born a few moments later, proved to be extremely ugly. "Pray do not be too distressed, Madam," said the Fairy, "This daughter will have other compensations. She will be so intelligent that no one will really notice how very plain she is."

"I do *hope* so!" replied the Queen, "But can't you give just a little *sense* to the elder girl, who is so beautiful?"

"I can do nothing for her, Madam," said the Fairy, "at least as far as intelligence is concerned. But beauty is another matter. Since there is nothing I wouldn't do to please you, I will give her the power of making beautiful the person she likes best."

Everything turned out just as the Fairy had foretold: Agatha, the plain Princess, learned to read when she hardly seemed big enough to hold a book of fairy tales; but her sister Florentine – the beauty – could not get the knack of reading, at all. And even after she finally began to learn, she often turned two pages at once, and cried, "Something's wrong! Something has happened to my story!" until her tutor turned back a page for her. And she never really seemed to enjoy any form of study or reading.

When the two Princesses grew up, their qualities grew right with them. Everyone talked of the beauty of the elder girl, Florentine, and the spirited intelligence of the younger, Agatha. It must also be said that, unfortunately, their defects greatly increased with age, as well. The lantern-jawed Agatha became visibly more ugly from day to day.

Florentine became daily more stupid. Either she did not reply at all when something was said to her, or her reply did not match the question. Though there

was not a mean bone in her graceful body, Florentine
constantly and unknowingly offended those about
her. If a courtier came forward to introduce his young
sister, Florentine was sure to say something like, "Oh,

and is this your *mother?*" Luckily, everyone knew she had no malice, or there would have been hard feelings when she accepted a gift by saying, "Thank you for the necklace. I like it even if it is not as pretty as the one someone else brought me from Paris."

Florentine was as clumsy in actions as in speech, and was incapable of arranging so simple a thing as a few pieces of china on the mantelpiece without breaking at least one of them but this is not to say that Florentine did not try to improve.

When her father, the King, gave her an exquisite *nécessaire* – a little sewingcase to hang from her belt, with tiny scissors in it, and gold needles, miniature bobbins of silk thread, and a thimble studded with diamonds – she resolved to make him a present. Out of the finest linen, she stitched a shirt for her father, carefully, as she had been taught to sew. She would let no one see it as she worked, but secretly put all her best effort into the tight little seams. Unhappily, upon receiving this gift of love, to save his life the King could not pull the shirt on, for his beautiful addlepated daughter had fitted the sleeve directly to the neckband, and securely sewed the two together!

Although beauty gives a girl great advantages, the younger sister Agatha nearly always outshone her

elder sister in company. At first everyone clustered around the beautiful Florentine to look at her and admire her, but very soon they flocked instead around intelligent Agatha to hear the thousand amusing things she constantly said. It was amazing to see how in less than a quarter of an hour the beautiful girl would be quite deserted, while everyone now surrounded the younger sister.

Although the older girl was stupid, she was well aware of this, and would have given all her beauty, without a moment's regret, in exchange for half her sister's liveliness and wit. She walked in the royal rose garden, and as she walked, the Venetian lace of her overskirt caught upon a thorny branch. Her sister Agatha would have stooped to loose the delicate fabric. But not Florentine. When she felt the slight pull of lace, she kept on walking until a great tear had ruined her overskirt. The Queen was a kind woman but this sort of thing drove her distracted. "How *can* you be so unmindful, Florentine? So utterly stupid!" The poor foolish Princess almost died of chagrin.

One day, hardly noting where her steps took her, the Princess Florentine took refuge in a wood to bewail her misfortunes. Suddenly she saw, coming

90

towards her, a little man, most ugly and unattractive but magnificently dressed. It was the young Prince Ricky, who had fallen in love with her from her portrait which was to be seen everywhere, and he was on his way to her. He had left his father's kingdom especially to have the pleasure of meeting her and taking to her.

Delighted to find her alone like this, he went up to the Princess Florentine with all possible deference and courtesy. After paying her the usual compliments, he noticed how sad she was and said to her, "Madam, how can someone as beautiful as you appear so melancholy? Let me tell you that I have seen an infinite number of beautiful women. My father's court swarms with them. Yet I have never seen one whose beauty could approach yours."

"You think so, Sir?" the Princess Florentine replied. She said nothing more, and did not smile in return to his smile.

"Beauty," continued Prince Ricky, "is so great an advantage that it makes all others unnecessary. When one is beautiful, how can anything distress her very much?"

"I would much rather be as ugly as you are, Sir, if I could be as smart," said the Princess, "than to be as good-looking and yet as ridiculous a fool as I am."

"There is no surer sign of a person's intelligence, Madam, than the belief that he is not intelligent. It is the very nature of that gift that the more we have of it, the less of it we believe we have."

"I don't know about that," replied the Princess, "but I do know that I am remarkably stupid. Everybody tells me so – and *I* see it, too. It makes me so sad that I shall surely die of mortification and unhappiness."

"If being stupid is all that distresses you, Madam, I can quite easily cure your sorrow," said the Prince assuredly.

"And how can you do that?" asked the Princess.

"Dear Princess," replied Prince Ricky, "I have the power of bestowing the highest possible degree of intelligence on the one I love most. Since you, Madam, are that person, the highest possible degree of intelligence is yours – if only you will marry me."

The Princess was astounded. She stared dully at the Prince, and did not reply.

"I can see," Prince Ricky went on, "that this proposal does not seem to charm you, and I am not surprised ... Well, I will give you a whole year to get used to the idea."

The Princess had such an overwhelming anxiety to be sensible and bright, and so little awareness of time, that "a whole year" sounded to her like "until the end of the world." She thought the end of a year would never really come. The result was that Princess Florentine at once accepted the proposal of Prince Ricky.

No sooner had she promised Ricky that she would marry him one year from that very day than she felt completely changed. She discovered that she had an incredible facility for saying exactly what she wanted to say, and for saying it easily, agreeably and naturally. She immediately began an animated conversation with Prince Ricky. "Now, where did you see my portrait, and decide we should meet?" she asked.

"Dear Lady, the Queen, my mother, has a thousand little boxes – gifts from her ill-favored son, who likes to frequent the country fairs – all with your likeness on them. In every shop and wayside booth, the makers of pomades, pomanders, perfumes and potions make sure to sell their fragrant wares by attaching your lovely countenance to them. There is no corner high or humble where your sweet face is not known."

At this explanation, the Princess Florentine smiled and began to tell Prince Ricky some of the silly things

she had done. She made the story of her father's shirt, for instance, so funny that he began to think he might have given her more intelligence than he had kept for himself.

When Florentine went back to the palace, the court did not know what to make of her sudden and extraordinary transformation. For every stupid remark that she had been heard to make previously, she now spoke directly to the point and with infinite wit. She took the hand of an elderly gentlewoman whose son had brought her newly to the Court, and delighted the visitor by saying with a twinkle, "You need not tell me, Lord Belfontaine, I can see you have brought your sister to meet us."

Everyone at Court felt pleased by signs of her tact – except the younger Princess, who was not at all pleased to have lost that intellectual advantage she had held over Princess Florentine, beside whom she now seemed only a dowdy wallflower.

The King began to let himself be guided by his elder daughter's advice, and sometimes held Councils of State in her apartments. Rumors of her transformation were heard everywhere, and all the young princes from neighboring kingdoms did their best to gain Princess Florentine's love, and most of them proposed. But not one of them was intelligent enough for her taste, and she listened to them all without accepting any.

However, there was one suitor who did seem so powerful, so rich, so witty and so handsome, that the beautiful Princess could not help feeling drawn towards him.

This young man also unfortunately had an extremely fine opinion of himself. Florentine's father noticed his daughter's interest in the self-admiring suitor, to whom he was not favorably inclined, but he said that he would leave her quite free to make her own choice of husband. She had only to say which one of all her suitors she wished to marry.

The more intelligent one is, the more difficult it is to reach a firm decision in such matters, so the Princess thanked her father and asked him to give her time to think it over.

In order to make up her mind undisturbed, she went walking. Quite by chance she chose to stroll in the very same wood where she had first met Prince Ricky. As she walked along, lost in thought, she heard a muffled noise at her feet, just as if a horde of people were coming and going and bustling about. She listened more carefully and soon began hearing voices saying, "Give me that casserole," and "Hand me that saucepan," and "Put some more wood on the fire," and many such instructions.

Suddenly the ground opened wide and Princess Florentine saw at her feet what seemed to be an enormous kitchen filled with chefs, scullery boys, and all the other people necessary for the preparation of a magnificent banquet. A group of twenty or thirty of those cooks who do the roasting marched out of the kitchen into one of the grassy avenues of the wood and crowded around a very long table. Each one had a larding needle in his hand. With their tall white chefs' hats bobbing up and down, they all set to work on the roasts, to the rhythm of a tuneful song.

The Princess, perplexed and amazed at this activity, called out and asked them whom they were working so hard for.

"Madam," replied the man who appeared to be the head-roaster, "we are working for our beloved Prince Ricky – the famed Esmond Riquet – who is being married tomorrow."

The Princess, more surprised than ever, remembered with a shock, that it was a year to that very day since she had promised to marry Prince Ricky. She was dumbfounded. The reason she had forgotten her promise was that when she made it, she had still been very stupid. The moment that the Prince's gift of intelligence had transformed her, her pleasure had driven all obligation out of her mind.

Soberly, she continued her walk and had barely gone another thirty steps when Ricky appeared before her, handsomely dressed, just like a Prince who is about to be married.

"Here I am, Madam," he said. "I have kept my word, and I see that you are here to keep yours – to make me the happiest of men by giving me your hand in marriage.

"Prince Ricky, you are mistaken. I must tell you frankly," replied the Princess, "that I haven't yet made up my mind about marrying, and when I do, I am afraid that I shall not make it up in the way you would like."

"You amaze me, Madam," said the Prince.

"I am sorry about this," the Princess went on, "and I realize that if I were dealing with a coarse and stupid man, I should be in a very difficult position. 'A princess has only her word of honor,' he would say to me, 'So you must marry me because you promised to do so'. But as I am talking to one who is a man of the world, and gifted with the highest intel-

ligence, I am sure that he will be more open to reason. You recall that even when I was stupid I was barely able to make up my mind to marry you. How can you expect me to arrive at such a decision *now*, when you have endowed me with so much intelligence that I am even more difficult to please? If you really wanted to marry me, you should not have cured my stupidity and made me able to see things more clearly than I once was able to."

"Madam," replied Prince Ricky, "If a man without intelligence would be justified – as you suggest – in reproaching you for not keeping your word, why should I not do the same, since my whole life's happiness is at stake? Is it reasonable that people of intelligence should be at a greater disadvantage than those without intelligence? Can you really maintain this, you who are now so clever and who so much wanted to be clever?"

"But let us come to the point, if you please," the Prince continued. "Apart from my ugliness, is there anything else about me that upsets you? Do you dislike my birth, for instance? Or my intellect? Or my character, or my manners?"

"By no means," replied the Princess. "I like you in all the respects you have just mentioned."

100

"If that is so," rejoined Prince Ricky, "I am going to be very happy, because *you* are able to make me the most attractive of men."

"How can *I* do that?" asked the Princess.

"To do it," replied the Prince, "you have only to like me enough to *want* to do it. Let me reassure your doubts, Madam: the same Fairy who on the day of my birth gave *me* the power to bestow intelligence on the person I most loved, gave *you* the power to bestow good looks upon the person you most loved – only if you really *wanted* to do so."

"If that is true," said the Princess, "I wish with all my heart for you to become the most dashing and attractive Prince in the whole world! I offer this gift to you as far as my power extends."

As the Princess was speaking these words, Prince Ricky – ungainly, slope-shouldered, long-faced, – came to be, in her eyes, the most fascinating, shapely, and attractive man in the whole wide world.

Some people say that it was not the power of the Fairy which worked this transformation, but the power of Love. They say that when the Princess reflected upon the perseverance of her lover, his tact, and all his fine qualities of mind and spirit, she no longer was aware of the deformity of his body or the ugliness of his face. His bowed back became the elegant gesture of a fashionable attitude. His limp, which had previously repelled her, now seemed no more than a becoming air of gravity which charmed her. They even say that she thought his frown made his eyes seem more dazzling; and she regarded the fact that one of his eyes was blue and the other brown, as a sign of Prince Ricky being a wonderfully uncommon being!

However this may be, Princess Florentine promised on the spot to marry Prince Ricky, provided that she could obtain the consent of her father, the King. Learning of his daughter's high opinion of Prince Ricky, and hearing also that he was most talented and upright in character, the King was delighted to accept him as a son-in-law. The wedding took place the next day, just as the Prince had planned and in accord with the arrangements he had made a long time before. And to the end of their happy lives, the Princess Florentine always said, "There is no one anywhere, like my own Ricky!"

Little

Red

Riding

Hood

Little Red Riding Hood

ONCE upon a time, in a village not too far from here, there was a little girl, one of the prettiest little girls imaginable. Her mother loved her dearly. Her grandmother, who loved her even more dearly, made her a little red cape with a hood. This cape was so becoming to the child, who wore it constantly, that soon everyone called her Little Red Riding Hood.

One day her mother baked some cakes and said to her, "I hear Grandmother isn't very well. You must go and see how she is. Get the wicker basket, and you can take her one of these cakes and this little bowl of fresh churned butter."

So Little Red Riding Hood and her mother put a nice white cloth into the wicker basket and carefully set a round sponge cake-with-a-hole-in-the-middle next to the little bowl of fresh churned butter.

"Be careful, my child. Go straight to Grandmother's and don't fiddle-faddle on the way. Your father is out hunting, and you may meet him. Keep to the main path, dear, and don't speak to strangers."

Little Red Riding Hood, with the wicker basket on her arm, set off at once to visit her grandmother, who lived in another village, across the woods.

What she did not know was that a certain wolf skulked in the woods, circling through its paths and hidden ways, hungry for a hen pheasant or whatever tasty tidbit he might find. As Little Red Riding Hood came skipping along, the wolf, who had sighted her red cape some distance away, stepped out from behind a tree.

"How do you do, my dear," he said, politely. "Haven't we met before? My name's Angus Wolf. What's yours?"

Little Red Riding Hood stood still for a moment.

"I'm called Little Red Riding Hood," she answered, "but I don't think we have met before."

"Well, we are friends now, aren't we, Red Riding Hood?" The wolf's hunger was so great – he had not had even a tough old rooster to eat these past three days – that he really was afraid Little Red Riding Hood would hear his stomach growl.

"What's in that basket on your arm, and where are you taking it, honey?" He would very much have liked to eat her up that instant, but he did not dare because he knew there were woodcutters nearby.

Little Red Riding Hood answered the wolf's question. "I'm going to see my grandmother. She's sick, and I'm taking her a cake-with-a-hole-in-the-middle and a little bowl of fresh churned butter from my mother."

"Does she live near?" asked the wolf.

"Oh, no," said Little Red Riding Hood. "She lives on the other side of that mill you can see over there – yonder, in the first house on the edge of the village."

"Well," said the wolf, "I think I would like to visit her, too. I'll take this road and you take that road, and let's see who gets there first."

The wolf ran off as hard as he could, by a short cut. Little Red Riding Hood took the longer road, and stopped here and there to gather nuts and run after butterflies and pick flowers that caught her eye.

In no time at all the wolf reached Grandmother's house. He tapped on the door with his paw. *Tap, tap*.

"Who's there?" called the grandmother from her bed.

"It's Little Red Riding Hood," said the wolf, trying to make his voice soft as a little girl's. "I have brought you a cake-with-a-hole-in-the-middle and a little bowl of fresh churned butter that my mother made for you."

Grandmother answered, "Pull the catch to lift the

latch, dear, and the door will open."

The wolf pulled the catch to lift the latch and the door opened. He grabbed the old woman and gobbled her up in one big gulp, for he had had nothing to eat these past three days. Then he hiccupped, because in his greed he had swallowed the grandmother whole.

He shut the door, pulled on Grandmother's ruffled cap and her long-sleeved nightgown, and climbed up into her high bed, to lie in wait for Little Red Riding Hood.

Sure enough, soon came Little Red Riding Hood, tapping at the door.

"Who's there?" he asked.

The deep gruff voice of the wolf surprised Little Red Riding Hood, but thinking that her grandmother must have a bad cold, she answered, "It's Little Red Riding Hood, Grandmother. I have brought you a cake-with-a-hole-in-the-middle and a little bowl of fresh churned butter that my mother made for you, and flowers I picked along the way."

The wolf tried to sound less gruff as he replied, "Pull the catch to lift the latch and the door will open, dear."

Little Red Riding Hood pulled the catch, lifted the latch and the door opened. The wolf had jerked

Grandmother's cap down over his ears the best he could, and had drawn the sleeves of the nightgown down over his paws. But the moment he saw Little Red Riding Hood in the doorway he slid down under the bedclothes, to hide. He lifted the corner of the quilt just enough to say, "Put the cake and the little bowl of butter on the bread-chest and come over here beside me, dear."

Little Red Riding Hood dutifully unpacked her wicker basket and then came over to the side of her grandmother's bed. But she was astonished at what she saw instead of the familiar, kind face under the ruffles of Grandmother's cap.

"Why, Grandmother, what big eyes you have!"

"All the better to see you with, my dear."

"And what big ears you have, Grandmother!"

"All the better to hear you with, my dear."

"But Grandmother – what big teeth you have!"

"All the better to *eat* you with, my dear!" And at that, the wicked wolf jumped at Little Red Riding Hood and gulped her down all in one swallow. Only her red cape was left on the floor.

Then the wolf, more than filled and feeling drowsy, eased himself back into the grandmother's bed and comfortably sank into a sound sleep.

The father of Little Red Riding Hood had been out hunting. His search for game brought him finally around to the edge of the village and Grandmother's house. So he stopped, knocked, pulled the catch to lift the latch, and opened the door to the sound of a wolfish snore.

Then he saw his child's red cape, and he knew what had happened. Quick as anything, with the sharp hunting knife that was in his belt, he laid that wicked wolf wide open. Out jumped Little Red Riding Hood and the kind Grandmother. They all hugged each other joyfully – the grandmother, the father, and Little Red Riding Hood.

Her father pulled the wolf outdoors to skin him, and the grandmother said to Little Riding Hood, "Where's that nice cake-with-the-hole-in-the-middle? Let's all have a great big piece!"

So they did, and then Little Red Riding Hood's father took her safely home.

There is no longer a wolf in that forest, but now Little Red Riding Hood takes no chances. She keeps to the path, leaves the flowers and butterflies where they are – and never speaks to strangers.

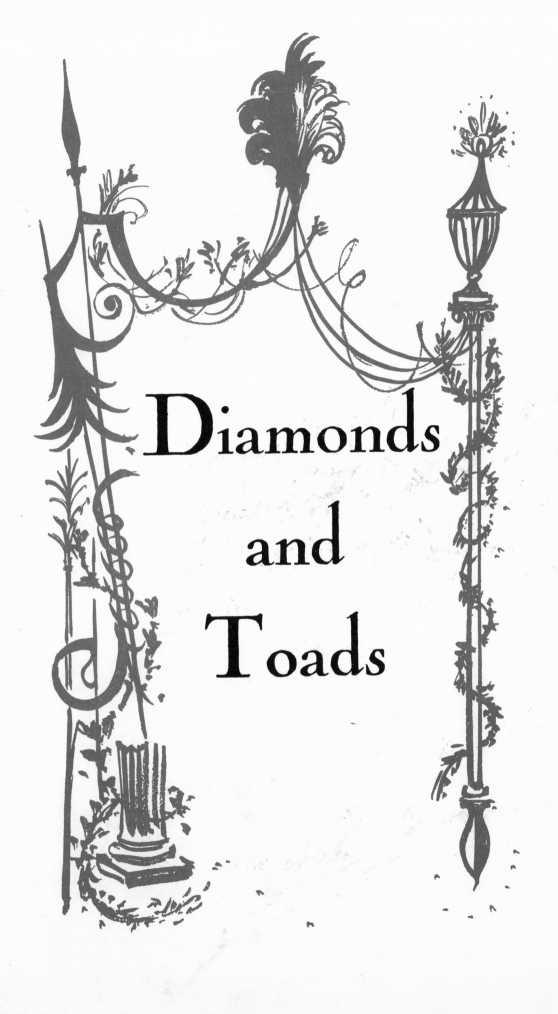

Diamonds
and
Toads

Diamonds and Toads

ONCE upon a time there was a widow who had two daughters. The elder daughter, a most disagreeable girl, looked and acted just like her mother. In fact, both the mother and the daughter were so unpleasant and arrogant that no one could bear them. The younger girl resembled her father in gentleness of conduct and goodness of heart. Besides, she was one of the most beautiful creatures you ever saw.

Since it is natural for people to love and admire what is most like themselves, the mother loved the elder daughter with all her heart, but she detested the

117

younger one. She made her eat alone in the kitchen, and obliged her to work all the time.

Besides doing the sweeping and scrubbing, the sewing and mending, the cooking and serving, the poor younger daughter, Rosemary, had a special chore: every day she had to trudge twice to a well a mile from the house and carry back a heavy pitcher of water. One morning when she was at the spring, a shabby old woman hobbled up to her.

"I'm thirsty this hot day, dearie. Would you let me have a drink out of your pitcher?"

"Yes, of course I will, good mother," said Rosemary, and rinsing out the pitcher, she dipped it into the coldest, clearest part of the well. She offered it then to the old woman, and held up the heavy pitcher so that the old woman could drink without spilling.

When the old woman had slaked her thirst, she smiled gratefully and then said to the girl, "You are so beautiful, so kind, and so compassionate that I mean to give you a present." She was a Fairy, and had taken on the form of a poor village woman, in order to find out just how kindhearted Rosemary was.

"The gift that I am giving you," continued the Fairy, "is that every time you utter a word there will

come out of your mouth a flower or a precious stone."
Then the Fairy vanished.

When Rosemary reached home, her mother
screeched at her for taking such a long time.

"I'm sorry to have been so long, Mother," the girl
apologized. As she spoke, the magic began – two roses,
two pearls, and two large diamonds fell from her lips.

"Goodness me!" exclaimed her mother in astonishment. "I do believe all sorts of diamonds and
pearls are coming out of your mouth! What in the
world has come over you, dear child?" It was the

first time the mother ever had called her younger daughter "dear child".

In perfect trust, the girl told her story – and of course a whole heap of gems piled up as she spoke, diamonds and rubies dropping to the floor at every word.

"Well, I never saw anything like this in all my life," said the mother. "I really must have your sister go for the next pitcher of water."

She called to the odious elder one. "Look, Fanchon! Come see what marvelous treasure comes from Rosemary's mouth when she talks. Wouldn't it be wonderful if *you* had the same gift? All you have to do is to go draw water at the well and when a poor old woman asks you for a drink, you give it to her as politely as you can. Isn't that easy?"

"Catch *me* going to the well!" retorted the rude girl.

"You most certainly *will* go," her mother replied, "and you'll start right this minute!"

So off she went, grumbling and muttering every step of the way, swinging by its handle the handsomest silver pitcher her mother owned. No sooner had she reached the well than out of the neighboring wood came a fine lady dressed in elegant clothes.

"My throat is parched with the heat of this day. Will you please give me a drink from your pitcher?" she said. It was the same Fairy who had appeared to the younger sister, but this time she had put on the dress and manner of a Princess, in order to discover the true quality of the older sister.

"You have your nerve! Anyone might think I brought this good silver pitcher all the way out here just for *you*!" sneered the girl. "As if I came here to give drinks to fine ladies! If you're thirsty, draw your own water from the well, and slurp it out of your hands."

"You are not very polite," said the Fairy, quietly. "I have a suitable present for such a disobliging, ungenerous girl: every time you speak, either a snake or a toad will fall from your mouth." And the Fairy disappeared.

As the ugly-spirited girl turned back toward home, her mother ran out to meet her.

"Well, Daughter," her mother began in eager anticipation.

"Well, Mother," mocked the disagreeable Fanchon – and with her first words, two snakes and two toads fell from her mouth and made away into the grass.

"Goodness me!" screamed the mother. "What in

the world has gone wrong? Oh, this is all your sister Rosemary's fault! I'll teach her!" And off she ran to give the younger daughter a beating.

Driven from the house, the younger daughter took refuge in the woods. The King's son, as he returned from hunting, met her and asked her why she was alone in the woods, crying.

Rosemary curtsied, spreading her torn apron with the grace of a highborn lady in a rich gown. "Alas, sir," she said, "My mother has driven me out of our house."

Observing her beauty, and the diamonds that sprang from her lips, the King's son asked her to tell him how she, in her poor rags, could produce such jewels. She told him all that had happened, and, listening, the King's son fell in love with sweet Rosemary. And since her magical gift from the Fairy would more than match any wedding dowry he could receive from another bride, of his father's choice, he took her home to the palace and there he married her.

As for the arrogant older sister, she made herself so disagreeable that at last her own mother could no longer endure her. The time came when the two of them parted company, and the elder sister went to live alone in a corner of the woods with her toads and vipers.

The
Three
Wasted
Wishes

The Three Wasted Wishes

ONCE there was a Woodcutter who worked very hard every day. He felt very discontented as he swung his ax and felled tree after tree, day after day. He took to complaining all the time. One day, as he was grumbling to himself, "I never have any luck. Why can't something wonderful ever happen to me? Nothing I've wished for *ever* came true. I might as well be dead," his complaints were overheard by the god Jupiter.

Jupiter was taking one of his occasional strolls down from Olympus, his thunderbolts in hand. He made himself visible to the Woodcutter, who immediately fell down, abject and frightened. "I take back everything I said, Your Worship," he quavered. "I didn't mean a word of it! I don't wish anything. I'll give up wishing altogether, if you'll just stop your thunder."

"You need not be afraid," Jupiter assured the Woodcutter good-humoredly. "No harm will befall you. I have heard your complaints and I am here to show you how wrongly you think of me. Far from balking your desires, I shall further them. I, master of the universe, promise you that you shall have the next three wishes you make, no matter what they are . . . Better think carefully, before you make them, to be certain of what will give you most happiness." And in a clap of thunder, Jupiter was gone.

The Woodcutter cut no more wood, but, shouldering his ax, turned lightheartedly toward home. "Wait until I tell Matilda!" he thought. "Now the little woman and I can improve the cottage, and maybe buy a cow. Or I might get a whole farm and give up woodcutting. We could get ourselves one of those cozy little narrow houseboats, and spend our time on the canals, going through the locks and enjoying the green countryside, just lying in the sun and watch-

ing other people work. Or we could . . ." and he went on and on, thinking up things they could do with no expense to themselves, until he reached his home.

"Hey, Mattie!" he called to his wife, as soon as he had put away his ax. "Serve up the soup! Let's put another log on the fire. Throw the dog a bone, and pour the cat some milk. We're going to be rich! All we have to do is to make three wishes, and anything we want is ours."

The little woman, who towered over her husband, the Woodcutter, listened greedily as he related all that had passed between him and Jupiter. As the Woodcutter began to speak of their buying a cow or becoming gypsies or drifting through the waterways, the good woman, who had quite different and fancier ideas, stopped him.

"Just a moment, please! Remember, easy does it, Blaise. Let's think this over carefully and make no mistakes. Perhaps we had better sleep on it, and decide tomorrow what we want for our first wish."

"You are right!" her husband agreed, "But in the meantime, why don't you go down to the cellar and draw us some of that wine we've been saving for a celebration?"

When his wife brought back the wine, the Woodcutter drank deeply, and leaned back in his chair to enjoy the fire. "What we could use with this now, Matilda, is a delicious long sausage. Umm-m, I wish we had one."

Instantly, a long red sausage flung itself out of the air from nowhere and thumped down onto the table at the Woodcutter's elbow.

His wife, seeing that this was the answer to the first wish – the wish her husband had made without even thinking – shouted, "You idiot! You've wasted the first wish!" She began to bawl. "We could have had anything in the world," she sobbed, "– a king's palace, wheelbarrows full of diamonds and opals, paisley shawls, a coach and horses, gold dishes – and *you*, you simpleton, *you* had to wish for a sausage!"

Now the Woodcutter was already vexed with himself for having let this silly wish slip into words. But he felt even more vexed with his wife for being right. As she continued to rave and berate him, he kept quiet until he could no longer hold in his anger, then howled, "I wish that accursed sausage were hanging on your nose!"

Immediately, the sausage leaped up from the table and attached itself to Matilda's nose. What a sight – the long red sausage dangling from the end of her nose! It did not add to the beauty of the good woman, though for a few startled moments it did prevent her from saying a word – an effect that pleased her husband.

Then the wife renewed her weeping. "*Now* what are you going to do? You've wasted our second wish and you've made a fool of me!"

"Well," her husband suggested, "we could still have that palace you were mentioning. I wouldn't mind being a *king*. Or we could . . ."

"Don't you dare! Never mind about kings or queens or anything but *me!* Get this sausage off my nose!"

The Woodcutter sighed. "Ah, but there's only one wish left, Tildie. We could be *rich*. Are you sure that all you want is just to look like other people?"

His wife took a threatening step towards him.

"All right! All right!" he said quickly, and drew a deep breath. "I wish," he said solemnly, "the sausage were off the end of my wife's nose."

Instantly the sausage disappeared.

The Woodcutter looked at his wife, and his wife looked at him. They had had their three wishes.

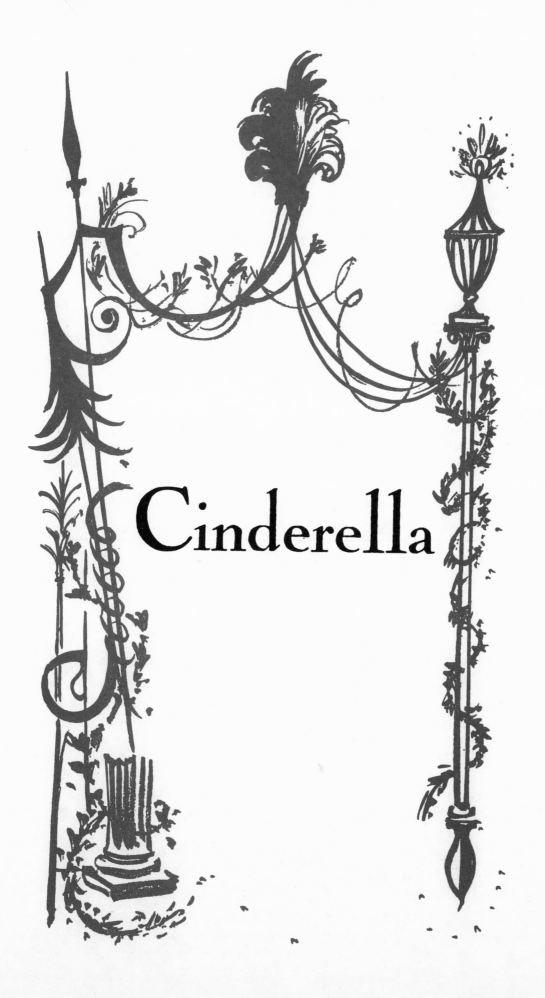

Cinderella

Cinderella

ONCE there was a highborn gentleman who took for his second wife the haughtiest and most disdainful woman to be imagined. Nothing was good enough for her and hers. She had two extremely plain daughters, Flaminda and Hortense, who were just like their mother in character and in their mean ways. They had nothing to recommend them. Their only talent was sneering, and at that, it must be admitted, they were experts. They even sneered at each other.

The nobleman had a daughter of his own, gently bred and tenderly brought up by her mother, his

beloved first wife, who had died a short time before. This sweet girl inherited the goodness of her mother, who had set a wonderful example of patience and kindness to all who knew her.

But the wedding bells had scarcely stopped pealing for her father's second marriage, the ceremony was hardly over, before the stepmother showed who was going to direct the household! She could not endure seeing her husband's daughter enjoying the same things as her own girls, so she gave her a new role.

"Don't think, Miss, that *you* are to sit around all

day in your best clothes and sip tea, or that guests and parties and carriages are for the likes of *you*. Down to the kitchen with you!"

She handed the frightened girl a faded and patched work-apron, and set her to work at all the household chores of cleaning and polishing and pot-scouring, so that the stepmother could spend all her time at pleasure and traveling.

Her husband had no idea what was going on, and if his daughter had complained to him that she was mistreated, he would not have believed it could be so, for he took his new wife's word for everything.

Because the poor sad girl sometimes sat wearily in a corner of the kitchen hearth among the cinders, which was the only warmth she could find in that house, her stepsisters made up a name for her. Flaminda, the older one, called her "Cinderbutt", and the younger and slightly softer-hearted sister called her "Cinderella". In any case, they both intended to keep her reminded always of her lowly position among the cinders.

Cinderella swept and cleaned their rooms, shook the curtains of their new silk-canopied beds, and smoothed their linen sheets. She, who had once had the same comforters of satin filled with goose-down,

138

now was made to sleep in the attic, with a mattress of corn shucks under her, and a moth-eaten old carriage robe for a cover. Her stepsisters had full-length mirrors on their walls – the better to study their own sour looks. The placid brook or a bowl of water provided Cinderella with her only mirror, yet she was as lovely as the morning.

One fine day the King's son gave a ball, to which the young persons of all the noble families were invited. It was understood – by those who gave the matter any real thought – that the ball would make it easy for the Prince to have a careful look at all the most beautiful damsels of the kingdom, for it was time that he should marry. And while he was surveying the prettiest girls, his courtiers, too, might see them and be seen – and pick out their wives-to-be. So every young lady began to plan her costume, and the stepsisters were no exception. (They had, of course, received invitations, for their family was an important one.)

"What shall we wear?" they asked each other, holding up one dress after another, as they swished back and forth in front of the long mirrors.

"Cinderella, heat the iron and crimp the ruffles on this sleeve!" called Flaminda.

"Cinderella, take a needle and sew this lace around my collar!" ordered the other stepsister.

"I think I'll put on my yellow velvet with the black stripes running crosswise," decided Flaminda. "Don't you think it's dramatic, Cinderella?" The stepsisters knew that Cinderella had good taste, and though they might insult her, they did want her to think they looked stylish.

"You look fat as the pig you are," snapped Hortense at Flaminda, before Cinderella could answer.

"Perhaps if the stripes ran up and down, instead of around," murmured Cinderella.

"Nothing of the kind! You're just jealous cats, both of you," retorted the older sister. "The yellow and black it shall *be*! You've made up my mind for me!"

"Well," said the younger one, "*I* mean to wear my paneled skirt with twelve crinolines under it, and my red-lined cape. And I shall show off my gold bracelets – the whole collection – clear up to my elbows. *That* will give the Prince something to look at!"

"Yes, it will," agreed Flaminda. "*Anything* to keep him from noticing that long nosey nose of yours!"

Before they could fly at each other, Cinderella interrupted gently. "How will you do your hair? High, in pompadour fashion?"

Yes, yes, that was *just* how they would have it up! Call in the fussiest, fanciest hairdressers! Get their Spanish combs. Hortense would have no less than six large combs stuck into her heaped-up frizz. "Pierced tortoise-shell – that costs the most. I'll have what is most expensive – and lots of it," she announced.

"Hortense is so showy," sniffed Flaminda. "Cinderella, let the chaffinch out of his cage. I mean to comb my hair high up over it. No – wait. Leave the bird *in* his cage. I shall draw my hair up over the back and sides, and in front everyone can see the pretty little gold wires of the cage and hear the song of the bird inside. *There's* a clever note!" She smirked with satisfaction.

Cinderella did whatever the sisters wanted, running up and down, in and out, hither and yonder, helping the girls in a thousand ways, as they changed their minds and flung aside one garment after another.

This hubbub went on for days. The sisters asked Cinderella her opinion of this and that, and accepted her judgments, which they knew were honest. But their own mean nature broke through and one day made them say to her, "*You* ought to be going to the ball, too. Would it interest you to come along?"

"Of course it would interest me! I'd *love* to go. But

you don't think they'd let me in, do you?" Cinderella knew very well that the sisters were only jibing at her, but she wanted to hear their answer, nevertheless.

"Let you in? Oh, *certainly*! They'd have the heralds blow a fanfare and say, 'Here comes Miss Dirty-face Cinderella. Make way for the Lady Ashheap No-stockings!' You'd be the belle of the ball, the talk of the evening." And the stepsisters doubled up with laughter at their own cleverness.

With no resentment or sharp reply, Cinderella nodded in simple agreement. "You are perfectly right. It would be silly for me to dream of going."

She turned her attention to the next problem of the two who were invited to the ball – their beauty patches. The girls opened up the charming little boxes made of china or lacquered paper, touched finger to tongue, and lifted up one little black design after another.

"Do you think a crescent moon at the corner of my eye is as pretty as a little heart?" Flaminda wanted to know.

Her sister Hortense offered no help. "Do what you please. I mean to cover every one of my freckles with a different kind of beauty patch. And then I think I'll join my eyebrows together with a row of stars.

Cinderella, won't that be rather unusual?"

"Most unusual," agreed Cinderella. "But do you really *want* that many beauty patches? Isn't it more fashionable and nice to have just one, or may be two?"

"That's the *point*, you idiot! I *like* to have a lot of what everybody is wearing. If they're wearing two, *I'll* wear *twenty*."

"Yes, Hortense-portense," jeered her sister Flaminda, "and don't forget to put a patch on the end of your long nose!"

In the middle of this amiable kind of exchange, the young ladies got on with their plans for the ball. Cinderella helped them practice with their hair. Anyone else being so reviled and jeered at might have been tempted to make tangled rat's nests of their coiffures, but Cinderella did her very best for them.

The rival sisters were so excited that they could hardly swallow a bite the last two days before the great affair. They squeezed themselves into tight little corsets and in trying to cinch their waists smaller and smaller, they broke more than a dozen corset strings. From morning till bedtime they posed and primped in front of the mirrors.

When at last the great day came, it was Cinderella who handed the young ladies their jewels and their

beaded bags, their capes and gloves and fans. And away they whirled, to dazzle and be dazzled.

As they drove down the road with never a backward glance, Cinderella watched their carriage until it was no longer even a speck on the horizon. Then she looked down at her own ragged clothes. The tears rose to her eyes, and as she went slowly back to the chimney corner and the cinders, she began to cry with all her heart.

At that moment, a sweet voice said, "Cinderella, dear child, tell your Godmother why you weep?"

Cinderella, greatly surprised, looked up at the beautiful being, who was her Fairy Godmother. Her great gray eyes were kind, and shone even more than her sparkling robe.

"I wish I . . . I want to go to the . . . oh, I can't tell you," Cinderella sobbed.

But her Fairy Godmother could of course read her thoughts, so she said, "You would like to go to the ball. Isn't that it?"

Cinderella nodded. "Oh, yes, yes!" Then she put her hands over her face to hide the hopeless tears that kept on falling.

"Well, it's easy: just be an obedient girl, do what I tell you," said her Godmother comfortingly, "and

I shall see that you have a way to go. First of all," she went on, "see if you can find me a well-shaped pumpkin in the garden."

Cinderella hurried into the kitchen garden, and quickly cut off the best-formed pumpkin on the vine. How it would help her get to the ball being given by the King's son she could not guess, but she took it back to her Fairy Godmother. Cutting away the stem part, the Fairy Godmother scooped out the seeds, leaving the hollow rind. Then she carried it out to the road, touched it with the tip of her magic wand, and presto! it turned into a magnificent gilded coach, with grand flourishes of crimson velvet on the seats and walls inside.

"Now where's the mousetrap I saw hereabouts? Ah – here it is, with six lively mice anxious to run outside! Open the door of the trap so that one mouse at a time can make his exit, and you shall see what happens."

Cinderella did exactly what she said. The Fairy Godmother touched her wand to each mouse as he scuttled through the little door. Immediately it turned into a handsome gray horse, until there in front of them stood a team of six fine horses to pull the resplendent coach!

When the Fairy Godmother paused for a moment, thinking how she would contrive a coachman, Cinderella said, "If there is a rat in the rattrap, might he not be good for a coachman?"

"You're right!" said the Fairy Godmother. "Go and see."

Cinderella went to get the rattrap. It had three rats in it – big ones. The Fairy Godmother picked the one with the longest, silkiest whiskers. One tap of her magic wand, and there stood a sturdy coachman, ready to crack his whip and drive off to the ball.

Then the Fairy Godmother said, "Go into the garden again, Cinderella dear, and behind the watering - can you will find six lizards. Put them into your apron and bring them to me."

No sooner said than done. Cinderella brought the lizards and in a twinkling the Fairy Godmother had turned them into six fine footmen. They mounted nimbly into their places on the coach, and anyone seeing them there in their brilliant liveries would have thought they had served as footmen all their lives.

Then the Fairy said to Cinderella, "Your carriage awaits – to take you to the ball. Are you happy now?"

"Yes, kind Godmother. But how will I look in these wretched rags? I won't even be let in!"

Then the Fairy Godmother made a circle in the air with her wand and touched Cinderella. Instantly her rags turned into a dress of shimmering gold, its bodice frosted with jewels.

"Look at yourself in the full-length mirrors," said the Fairy Godmother, and as Cinderella stared at herself, her hairstyle too was magically transformed. She seemed a princess!

"But, dear Godmother," said Cinderella hesitantly, "must I go *barefoot*?"

The question was hardly asked before the girl found herself wearing the most marvelous little slippers ever seen – of a sort that no one in all the world had ever worn: magical slippers of genuine glass!

As Cinderella happily stepped up into her splendid coach, her Godmother gave her a warning good-bye.

"Dear girl," she said, "your finery and coach will last *only until midnight*. Listen for the chiming of the clock, because, unfortunately, when the witching hour is struck, my magic ceases and you must be home. Stay even one minute past twelve and, to my sorrow, your coach will turn back to a pumpkin, the coachman will become a gray rat again, the horses will return to mice, and you will have no more footmen, because they will be lizards once more – and the guests at the ball will see you in your Cinderella rags."

Cinderella promised her Godmother faithfully to leave before midnight and then drove away to the ball, full of happiness.

The Prince had met a hundred or so young ladies at the ball that evening. Each gave him her deepest curtsy, her most engaging smile, the most flirtatious flutter of her eyelashes – for each young lady hoped the Prince might choose her for his Princess. But though he bowed and kissed each lady's hand, because that was custom and good manners, the Prince felt restless, almost bored. He had found no special One among the Many.

So when he heard that a lovely Princess – a stranger, unknown in these parts – had just drawn up in an elegant coach, the Prince ran out to welcome her himself, and offered her his hand.

As he led her into the royal ballroom, the guests stopped dancing to turn and see who had come. The women gasped at her shimmering gown; all the gentlemen wished they might dance with her. A low murmur rippled through the crowd: "How beautiful she is!" Even the old King, the father of the Prince, sat up and took fresh interest in the ball. "That's a very charming girl, m'dear," he confided to the

Queen. "I haven't seen her like in a long time. In fact," he added quickly, "not since *you* were her age, my dearest love."

The ladies busily studied the cut of Cinderella's costume, fixing it in their minds so that in the morning they could have one made just like it – if they could find any such gauzy cloth and any dressmaker clever enough to sew it.

The young Prince led his mysterious guest to the place of honor, and asked her what music she would like the court musicians to play. He was delighted to find her a flawless partner for the minuet, the gavotte, the saraband, the quadrille, the polonaise, the what-you-will. She skilfully threaded every maze of the dance, going away, coming back, and smiling up into the eyes of the captivated Prince as he took her hand.

Her stepsisters, Flaminda and Hortense, stared at Cinderella just as everyone did. But they did not recognize her – nor dreamed that they ever had seen her before.

Later on, supper was served – every course the work of a master chef. But the Prince could not eat for feasting on Cinderella's beauty. With a little pearly knife he cut a Spanish orange for her, scoring the peel in sections and pulling it back so that she might hold the fruit in her hand. Cinderella turned to her stepsisters who sat nearby, and offered them a share of the orange and some fragrant citrons. They gaped and said their thanks, but they did not recognize her at all.

Suddenly, as Cinderella spoke with the Prince, she heard the clock strike a quarter to twelve. Immediately she made a deep bow to the assembled company, and, before anyone could move to go to her, she had flown down the stairs and into her waiting coach.

Once home, she hastened to thank her Fairy Godmother, who waited by the kitchen fire. She described all that had happened, and told her Godmother of the second ball which was to be on the next night.

"The Prince begged me to come back, dear Godmother."

"And what did you say?"

"I did not know what to say until I could talk with *you*. I told him I would see."

"Good girl." The Fairy Godmother smiled.

At that moment the two stepsisters knocked at the door. Cinderella, back in her familiar rags, as she had been since the clock struck midnight, let them in. She yawned and stretched and rubbed her eyes as if

152

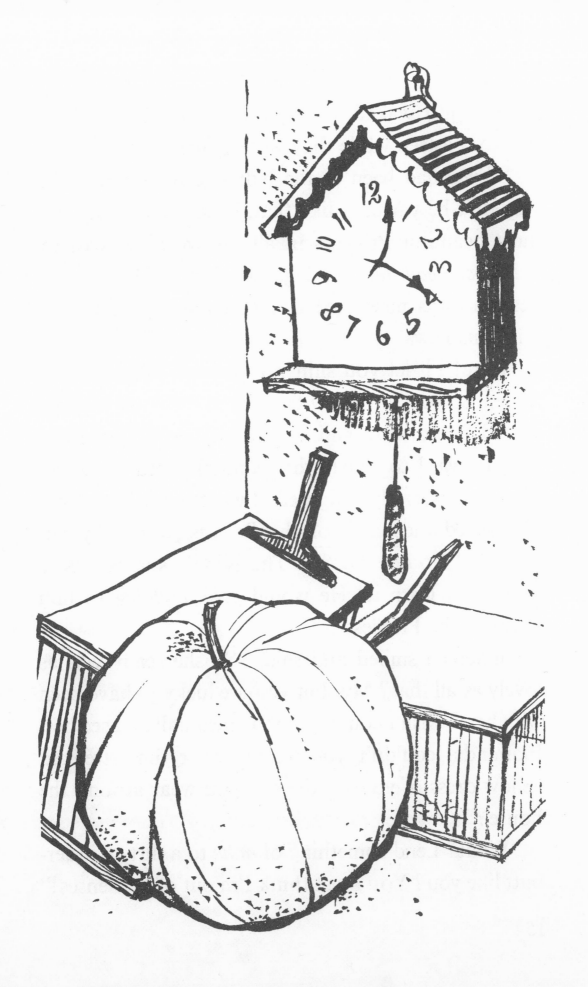

she had just waked, (though she certainly had been far from asleep while they were at the ball).

"If *you* had been at the ball where *we* were, you wouldn't be yawning like that, believe *me*! Why, the most beautiful Princess in all the world was there, *the most beautiful!* And guess whom she liked the best and was nicest to! Us!" Flaminda gave Cinderella this news.

"Here! I'll let you sniff my fingers," offered Hortense, "so you can know that the mysterious Princess shared her orange and citron with us." Cinderella bent forward to inhale the wonderful orange scent.

She was secretly delighted at what she was hearing. She asked the name of the Princess, but they answered, "No one knows. The King's son is beside himself to learn it! He would give *anything* to find out who the Princess is."

Cinderella smiled and said, "So she really was as lovely as all that? My, but you are lucky to have been with her. I wish *I* could go to the next ball and see her. Flaminda, couldn't you let me wear that streaked yellow dress of yours – the one you wear around the house?"

"What? Lend something of *mine* to a dirty Cinderbutt like you? You must think I'm out of my senses!"

154

And she flounced off to bed.

Cinderella had known this was the answer she'd get. She was glad of the refusal, because she would have been in a pretty pickle if her stepsister had been willing to lend the dress.

Next day the two stepsisters sallied off to the ball, and after they left, Cinderella went, too, in the gilded coach, as before. But her costume was even more dazzling than the first one. The young Prince seized her hands and stayed beside her all the evening long. "Tell me who you are, and promise me you will not run away," he begged. "I have not been able to think of anything or anybody except you since we met! Tell me your name. I love you!"

Cinderella found this sort of conversation so charming that she quite forgot to think about the passage of time. She suddenly became aware that the clock was striking the first chime of midnight when she thought it was not yet eleven! Without curtsying or waiting to excuse herself, she fled as lightly as a fawn down the long stairway. The Prince followed eagerly but was too far behind to catch her. In her haste, Cinderella lost one of her glass slippers, and dared not stop for it.

The Prince picked it up tenderly, and ran on. He

called to the palace guards to ask which way the Princess had gone. Alas, they told him that they had seen no princess. No one had passed through the gates, they said, except a girl in ragged work-clothes. No guest from the ball had left through the gate, they were certain.

Even as they talked, Cinderella was running breathless to her house, for as her Godmother had warned, no coach had been waiting to carry her. A pumpkin shell had rolled across the courtyard cobbles as she, holding her one glass shoe in her hand, had run past. Nothing was left of all her finery except this little glass slipper, the mate to the one she had lost.

When the two stepsisters returned from the ball, Cinderella asked them if they had had as fine a time as at the first ball, and if the unknown beauty had appeared again. They said that the lady had come, but that at midnight she had vanished more swiftly than on the previous evening.

"She lost one of her glass slippers," Hortense exclaimed excitedly, "and when we all saw how the Prince treasured it, we knew he must be in love with its owner."

The sisters had guessed right, of course. A few days after the ball, the King's son sent out his heralds

far and wide to proclaim throughout the land that he
wished to marry the lady whose foot belonged in the
little glass slipper.

His ambassadors went about with the slipper,
trying it on ladies according to their rank, the princesses first and then the duchesses, and then the ladies-
in-waiting, but with no success. Most of these females
could not force in so much as their great toe. After
all, the glass slipper was a magical one, made by the
Fairy Godmother of Cinderella, and could fit only her.

No wonder that when the heralds came to the
stepsisters, who tugged and grunted to push their
feet into the shoe, they also had no success. Cinderella, looking on, recognized her own slipper, and
said, with an apologetic laugh – almost as if it were
a joke to think of such a thing, "May I see if the shoe
will fit *me*?"

Her stepsisters stopped rubbing their bruised feet
in order to sneer at Cinderella. "Look who's trying
to be a Princess now!" they jeered.

Nevertheless, the courtier who was trying on the
slipper looked quickly at Cinderella and saw that she
was a beautiful girl. Since his orders were to try the
slipper on every foot, he asked Cinderella to sit
down and take her turn.

The glass slipper slid onto her little foot at once as she knew it would. And the astonishment of the two staring sisters became greater still when Cinderella drew from her pocket the mate to the lost shoe and put it on her other foot.

At that instant, the Fairy Godmother appeared, and by touching Cinderella with her magic wand, she transformed her again into the vision of loveliness she had been at the ball. The sisters realized that their slavey was really the Princess whom the Prince sought. They threw themselves at her feet and asked her to forget the ugly things they had said to her and the mean behavior they had shown her.

Cinderella, who could not cherish a grudge, raised her stepsisters up and told them she only wished that they should all be friends forever.

She was led by the heralds to the Prince, in her beautiful robes. He thought her even more enchanting than he had remembered, and in a few days they married. The wedding was a great ceremony to which the whole kingdom was invited.

Cinderella, who was as generous as she was good to look upon, took her stepsisters to live in the palace, and found two noblemen to marry them, and they all lived happily ever after.